AF513535

UNHERD

KARTIKEYA LADHA

UNHERD

A TALE OF LOVE, WISDOM AND STRENGTH

Anecdote
Publishing House

Anecdote
Publishing House

Anecdote Publishing House
E-35-A, E Block, Gali No. 2, Ganesh Nagar,
Pandav Nagar Complex, Delhi - 110092

Published by Anecdote Publishing House
Copyright © Kartikeya Ladha

First Edition 2022

ISBN: 9788195890767

MRP: ₹ 350.00

All Rights Reserved.
No part of this publication may be reproduced, stored, in a retrieval system, or transmitted in any form, or by any means – electronic, mechanical, photocopying, recording or otherwise—without the prior permission of the publisher. Opinions expresses in it are the author's own. The publisher is in no way responsible for those.

Book Promoted and Marketed by Champ Readers Pvt. Ltd.
Edited by Radhika Jajoo
Cover by Meenal Goel
Printed by Nutech Print Services - India

Table of Contents

Introduction

Fierce and ruthless lawyer James Walsh has only one aim in life - to conquer New York City. He is determined to become the youngest, richest and best partner his law firm has ever seen. With his unlimited confidence, lack of emotions and a single-minded vision in life, there really is nothing stopping him.

His life wasn't always the same though. Born to an Irish Catholic mother and an Immigrant Indian father, James was brought up in a rough neighborhood in Queens. When his half absentee father passes away suddenly, he is forced to grow up and understand the realities of living in New York City on his mother's salary as a nurse. He very quickly understands the power of money and decides, at a very young age, to chase the 'American Dream'. Thus begins the grind to find success in the world of capital, not caring for what or who is lost in the process.

In the never ending race to success and money, he meets Veronica, who is equal parts sultry, aspiring and manipulative. She wants the same things in life as James and soon, they get married - not for love of course, but to build together a life of their dreams. Together, they are an unstoppable force to reckon with.

What happens, though, when the illusion James has tried so hard to sustain crashes in front of his very eyes? When he is forced to deal with his unhinged darkness, something he has been suppressing since childhood? When a mysterious younger woman, Jessica, enters his life and fills it with light? When she disappears out of the blue?

As James steps on a quest to find Jessica, he finds himself encountering mystical situations and individuals, all of whom point him towards his own true calling.

A trailblazing pursuit awaits as James learns to surrender his being to the anonymous calamities of what has now gripped his life. Follow James as he builds and loses in New York City and is carried to faraway lands of India in his quest to find answers.

This book is a tale of loving and losing, of understanding the darkness and light within us, of travel and adventure, and of the ways in which life can surprise, inspire and encourage if you allow yourself to dance to the tunes of life.

CHAPTER ONE

REMEMBERING HER TOUCH

Being with a woman I truly loved made me understand, for the first time in my life, the deepest, darkest parts of my own. For the first time, I was in love with a woman who held nothing back while loving me. She surrendered to my every breath and I to her soul. We both surrendered to the divinity within us and to the one within the other person. When we were together, our hearts and spirits were enduringly merged.

Every day with her seemed like eternity, where we took birth in the morning and after sharing our entire lives together – unconditionally loving and caring through the day, died together at night.

I didn't know the power love holds until I experienced it myself. Love is the most powerful force, one that has the potential to heal the most broken of souls. Love in its absolute purity, in its unconditional nature, can't be contained by our human vessels.

She entered my life to remind me of this power. Both of us had lived through many lifetimes before we were united. Our destinies had collided for us to engage with one another and elevate ourselves through unconditional love. I didn't have to think about whether I was in love or not - I just knew it, and so did she. We both knew that what was happening to us was beyond our control. We weren't acting per our mind's demands, but through our bodies and hearts.

Falling in love took me to spaces my heart had never been in. I was carried through multiple dimensions while experiencing this force. This was only because I was with a woman who would look deep into my eyes, utter the words, "I love you", and mean it with every fragment of her soul.

Whenever I would look into her eyes, the whole world would come to a pause. Whenever we touched, I felt a spark riding through my veins, as if my spirit was being ignited. Whenever our bodies met, it was always a cosmic state of being.

Merging with her was like uniting with God.

She came into my life as a teacher to help me grow my understanding of love and in the process, helped me let go of my barriers to experience life in its absolute form. I never knew that I could love someone so deeply and intensely.

My world had been shaken after meeting her. All that I thought I knew about women and love was being torn apart. Every layer of conditioning I had pertaining to love, and women, was breaking apart in a reckless storm. With her sinking deep into my body through her every touch, my sense of self was disintegrating. I was no longer abiding by the rules of our physicality but had chiselled past them to enter a vortex of abyss where nothing physical could exist.

My fears decayed as our bodies intertwined in a dream-like space. I was being born again with the touch of her lips. Our paths had collided to amplify our hearts and have us go through a spin of time.

When I first met her, I was barely attempting to live. I was passing through days wanting to just survive. The world seemed to solely exist inside the little bubble that I had created for myself. Beyond it, my soul was darkened to the possibilities of what could enliven my spirit.

Meeting her changed my life in ways I could never have imagined. I did not ever see myself being profoundly captured by the heart of another. But then again, I barely knew what was possible back then. All I knew were a fine set of guidelines, that had been indoctrinated in my being, for what I could and couldn't do. What I could and couldn't be. What I could and couldn't see.

I found her, only to lose her, and was guided on a path of burying my grave and rising from the dead.

My father, Kabir Ahmed, had immigrated to New York from India in 1969, before I was born. He had cut ties with our family in Gujarat and had left everything behind to start a new life in America. Throughout my life, there was never a mention of why he had left his family. It was an unspoken cartilage, for which I had neither asked nor received any explanation.

My father did all kinds of odd jobs in New York. Although he had great intellectual calibre, he was never able to stick to one thing. Maybe this was because of his intellect, as he got easily bored doing one thing and needed constant mental stimulation, or maybe this was because of his gypsy soul that never let him settle for any one thing in life.

He met my mother, Susan Walsh, an American woman, a few years after moving to America and they got married a few months after they met. This hurry to the altar had more to do with him wanting a green card than to do with love. It wasn't that he didn't love my mother, he just didn't have it in him to settle or commit. Throughout his marriage to my mother, he spent less time at home and more outside.

He was free spirited, and was lucky to be living in America at a time when people were starting to question things. His gypsy nature was what attracted my mother to him in the first place. He was a coloured man in America, living a free life, not afraid of being who he was. This also obviously got him into trouble most of the time.

My mother was very different from my father. A nurse by profession, she came from a working-class white family. Her parents were Irish Catholic, and she was raised in a very conservative environment. Growing up, she started feeling shackled by their thinking, and couldn't see herself abiding by their way of life. She distanced herself from them and wanted to raise children and have a family of her own.

My parents, even though they loved each other, couldn't stay together as their paths were distinctive. Their marriage lasted for about 10 years, after which they separated. My father was able to stay in the marriage for so long only because of my brother and I, but he could never really fit into society. There was something wild about him, something I could never understand as a kid.

After their divorce, my brother and I grew up with our mother in Queens, New York. Our father visited us quite frequently as he was very fond of us. He always came to visit after living in some new place in America. He was always moving. Changing jobs. Changing cities. Changing himself. None of us knew where he lived or what he did. There was something different, something new about him every time I saw him. I couldn't figure out what it was when I was little.

My mother raised both me and my brother Samir, all the while working a full-time job at a hospital. She was my hero. She raised us with so much kindness and strength. Her dedication as a nurse and a mother was so admirable that even as a child, I knew how lucky I was to be her son.

A couple of years after separating from my mother, my father died in a car accident. I was only 11 years old when it happened.

I still remember that day vividly. My brother and I were sitting on the kitchen table, watching mom cook, when the phone rang. My mother picked it up and a few seconds into the conversation, her face became solemn and her eyes sad. A few tears fell down her cheeks. We didn't know then what had happened, but we knew something was wrong.

Mother told us after the call ended. She was always very upfront and honest with us. She never treated us like kids.

My immediate reaction was of disbelief. Followed by grief, which transmuted into anger. I could not believe that he was no more. I was angry at him and at the world. In all the times he had gone away, I always knew that he would come back in a few days. I could not believe that I would never be able to speak to him or hug him. I was so angry that he would leave us like that, but also sad for him, that his time on Earth was cut short at such a young age.

I held my breath to hold all these intense emotions down. Feeling so many emotions at the same time scared me, made me feel vulnerable and out of control. I did not know how to breathe or how to deal with my grief. I also needed to step up and be there for my brother, whose grief was heart breaking to watch. I subconsciously bottled up all my anger, pain and grief. Something changed in me after that moment. It was almost as if I purposely chose to ignore what had transpired.

A part of me – the part that could love, laugh and cry freely - also died with my father. Whatever memories I had of him, I put everything in a box that day and buried it somewhere deep in my mind.

The hospital where my mother worked was in Manhattan, so she would commute every day between Queens and Manhattan. The neighborhood we grew up in was quite mixed, with people from different backgrounds and ethnicities living together. Because my mother would go to work, my brother and I were forced to grow up early in life so that we could take care of ourselves. She never treated us like children, and in the process, we were able to take individual responsibility for our lives from an early age.

My brother looked more Indian than me. Many people thought I was Italian, or somewhere from the Mediterranean region. My parents had given one child an Indian name and the other an American one. They named me, "James", and my brother, "Samir". Both of us grew up to be very distinct individuals.

Although very different from one another, Samir and I shared a bond unlike any other. A bond thicker than blood. I was very protective of Samir and treated him more like a son than a brother. I guess growing up without a father instigated me to act like one for Samir, who was a delicate soul and found the harshness of New York difficult to deal with. His brown skin and distinct name gave him more unwanted attention.

I was four years older than Samir, who got picked on by the boys in the neighborhood rather frequently. This continued until the day a fight erupted between me and the group of boys who bullied him. There were six of them in total, so I was obviously beaten quite badly, but nevertheless put up a tough fight. I had to be taken to the hospital, along with a few other boys I was able to land my punches on. Mother, who hated violence, was very upset with me that day. She made me promise, while I was laying on the hospital bed with bruises and bandages covering my body, that I would never get into a fight again. Samir was standing just next to mother when I made that promise. In Samir's eyes, I was a hero for standing up to the kids who used to trouble him.

There were many occasions when I came close to breaking that promise. We grew up in a neighborhood where most parents would be out working during the day and the kids would be on their own. The schools in our neighbourhood weren't good, and many kids would get involved in petty crimes from a young age. It wasn't a safe neighborhood, and all I wanted was to move out of there. That's what our mother wanted for Samir and me as well, but we could not afford to live anywhere else.

Whenever I got the chance to go to Manhattan with my mother, I jumped at the opportunity. I loved going to Wall Street and watching men, in professional suits, rushing through the streets of New York in their undying quest to make money. Money seemed to me like a beacon of hope through which I could erase the bondages of my life.

My father didn't have much, so he didn't leave us anything. And my mother didn't take anything from her family, so we were raised on a nurse's salary in New York. Having lived through the financial struggle of raising two boys, my mother was keen on us getting educated, so that we could live financially secure lives.

I opted to become a lawyer, which was lucrative, but soulfully discharging. My mother really tried to get my brother to go to college and eventually work a high paying job, but unfortunately, he wasn't able to make it through high school and ended up working all kinds of odd jobs, much like my father. Samir wasn't very street smart though and struggled to cope with the toughness of the world around him. He had a talent in painting - that's the only way he could express himself. But he couldn't survive as an artist and ended up moving from one job to the other.

I moved out of my mother's house in 1990, at the age of 18, to go to Columbia University to pursue an undergraduate degree in Economics and Political Science. I had been awarded a full scholarship and knew that this was my way out.

My mother, Susan, was very happy the day I got into Columbia. She was a proud mother. Going to college at that time was considered a big deal in America, especially for someone from our neighborhood. I was one of the few people in my entire neighborhood to have gotten into college. Most people couldn't get in, even if there was the rare chance that their parents could afford it. My mother didn't want my fate to be that of my father and so, seeing me excel in societal terms put her at ease.

I worked two jobs through college to support myself and studied diligently to make sure I graduate with honours and be a solid candidate for Columbia Law School, which was one of the best in the country. I attended it right after completing my undergraduate degree.

The internet started scaling exponentially in the US in the 1990s. The world was going to change forever. Globalization was shaping a new world with Asia growing in its influence. The rise of the internet was giving birth to tech companies, who were going to define the new world order.

I was submitting myself to the worldly games, while something in me was unfailingly being suppressed through it all. The fear of ending up like my father wasn't just customary to my mother, but also to me. In not wanting to be like him, I would readily dismiss anything that connected me with him.

There would be moments when I would lose my consciousness and arrive in a formless space, which couldn't be made sense of. I wouldn't remember anything whenever such events transpired. It was always a blank haze, where I would drop out of my consciousness for hours, and return not knowing what had happened, or even be aware of how much time had passed by. This would happen a lot when I was younger, but as I actively fought it, the regularity of such incidents reduced.

I never shared the occurrences of such "events" with anyone. I didn't know what others would think of them. More so, I didn't know what to make of them myself. So, I simply learned to live in denial and focused my attention on the things I wanted to accomplish.

Esteemed law firms hired top Columbia graduates every year even before they passed the bar exam, which is required in the US to legally practice law. I got a job offer from a reputed law firm and I joined it as soon as I could. My bosses were mostly Jewish, and they taught me a great deal about becoming a cut-throat lawyer.

The office of the law firm was located on Wall Street, and I got an apartment for myself just a few train stations up towards midtown. It was an upscale neighborhood, and I didn't mind paying a big chunk of my salary to be staying there.

I knew that to excel in New York City I had to start playing my cards right from the get-go. My intention was clear - to make a lot of money. I was driven and hungry to make that happen.

Son of an immigrant father and a working-class mother, I was now living the American dream.

A dream that unknowingly carried me away from the truths of what rested inside. It broke me to pieces, while solidifying my fight against myself.

Years started to go by in flashes as I worked day and night to secure a fortune for myself. I became distant from my mother and Samir, who was going through life working different blue-collar jobs, earning just enough to get by in New York. He also moved out from our mother's house at the age of 18 but was still living in Queens sharing an apartment with a bunch of people, who worked similar blue-collar jobs. He felt abandoned because of the path I had chosen, but he never voiced his feelings, as he knew how important it was for me to secure a financially stable life. I was so blind-sided by my hunger for making money that I didn't even think about him.

Our lives had taken different routes, where I did not want any aspect of my previous life to be a part of my new one. It was a deep reckoning in me where all I wanted was to have the lifestyle that I had always romanticized about as a child.

When I was able to afford a two bedroom, contemporary styled, luxury apartment in a newly designed building in Manhattan, my mother was its first visitor.

The apartment was on the 45th floor, overlooking the shining towers of Manhattan through a broadened glass window fixed adjacent to the living room and the dining space. I had an interior designer work on the apartment, who had me spend most of my initial salary on buying decorative hand-crafted furniture to create a sophisticated space that was appealing to a visitor's eye. I didn't hesitate while spending the money, as I knew that to reach the top, I had to think and act like a man who was already there. The apartment was less for myself and more to receive validation from other people, who could be impressed by my success and not second guess my origins. I didn't want my past to dictate my future, so I buried my old self the moment I left Queens.

When we are trying so hard to run away from our past, it does come to bite us in its unshakeable forms. And that is exactly what happened when mother visited me.

We were having dinner overlooking the estates of Manhattan, when my mother said to me, "I am so proud of you." It was a two-course meal of roast chicken and green beans brought from a high- end restaurant in Manhattan, where it took weeks to get a reservation. Thanks to the reputation of my law firm, I was able to get through their list. I had bought a bottle of expensive Italian red wine from Tuscany to complement our dinner.

"The chicken is melting in my mouth." Said my mother.
"They take days to prepare this chicken. It's from one of the best restaurants in Manhattan." I replied with a twinkle in my eyes.
"The wine tastes delightful with it", continued my mother.
"They know how to make good wine in Italy." I commented with a sense of pride in my voice.
"Look at you. All grown up and achieving these things in life.

Most people in our neighborhood can't even think of affording such a meal. I always knew you were special", gushed my mother.

"I don't want to talk about the people in that neighbourhood, mom. It's in the past. And we are here now. Can we just enjoy this moment?" I said to her, a little agitated.

"It's not in my past. I still live there." She said, "But, you are right. Let's not go there. Tonight, we are here to celebrate my son's achievements. My son, who I am so proud of."

Changing the subject, my mother asked, "So, are you seeing anyone?"
"Nothing serious, mom." I replied.
"Why don't you find a nice girl now? You have accomplished a great deal. Settling down may be a good thing." She continued.

"Not now." I said in a dismissive tone.

I was becoming arrogant with time. The weight of suppressing my emotions would always come out in a form of aggression that I utilized effectively at my job.

My mother left after dinner, and I sat through the entirety of that night, savouring the wine and letting my senses drool over the lucidity of the effects that were sparked in my mind.

I was 26 at the time, and the youngest senior associate of my firm. They hired only from Ivy league colleges. Few of the partners in the firm saw a lot of potential in me, when they came to hire at Columbia. One of them became my boss,

Adam Hoffman.

Adam took me in as his associate and as the years progressed, we became a powerful team, with a strong clientele and loads of money in the bank. Our drive to make money, but more importantly, to make something out of ourselves was what made us work well as a team. We were ruthless, aggressive, and hungry. We wanted it all. I, even more than Adam. He would say to me sometimes, "You need to take it easy, kid." And I would tell him with a smirk on my face, "I will take it easy when I am dead." My intentions were clear - I wanted to become the youngest partner of the firm.

Adam always used to say to me, "I see a lot of me in you, kid." He was a son of Jewish immigrants from Israel and grew up in Brooklyn. He left his faith and family in his late teens to pursue his ambitions.

Adam was one of the youngest partners at the firm and he said to me once, as we were having a celebratory drink late at night in his massive office after closing a tough case, "Let's see if you can beat me at becoming the youngest partner at this firm."

"I will." I replied with assurance in my voice.

He knew I meant it.

CHAPTER TWO

THAT BLONDE IN THE BLACK DRESS

It was the year 2002. We had entered a new century with the world changing dramatically. The dot com bubble had recently transpired, and the stock market had collapsed after highly speculating the newly founded internet companies. Valuations were at an all-time peak and investors were pumping money into internet companies without any remorse. The Internet was the next big thing and investors were keen on getting in the game.

I was approaching my 30th birthday when the dot com bubble burst, shaking the economy and shutting down many internet companies. Fortunately, as a highly effective lawyer, I wasn't affected much by the dot com bubble and still had a torrent of work to do. It was around that time when I met my future wife.

I had been with many women by then. Living in New York as a successful young lawyer meant that many women wanted to sleep with me. The Mediterranean shade of skin, complementary to the brownish-green eyes, an athletic physique and a confident, driven personality, was enough to have many women fall for me. But none I could love. However, being raised by a kind, single mother gave my brother and I clear instincts with regards to women. I never disrespected any woman I was with, even if we were together just for one night. I was always honest with them about my intentions.

I was too self-centred and arrogant to be able to see beyond the life that I was busy creating. I was overly consumed by a unilateral way of thinking, where my prime focus in life was my career. Romance, friendships and family took a back seat. I had grown up to become very detached from the heart. I was hollow from the inside and not even aware of it. I was feeding into the mindset of validation and constantly seeking approval of my peers. Women were just another piece in that story, one that helped fulfil bodily pleasures and nothing more than that.

I always liked being in control. It helped me break out of the times when I could feel myself losing consciousness. I hadn't had one of such "events" in the longest time because of my ability to stay in control. My childhood memories kept fading, and I wasn't becoming a product of my ancestry but of my current environment, which is what I thought mattered.

It was at a bar in the Lower East Side, when I first met Veronica – my future wife. My colleagues, Ben, Nate, and I were seated in a booth a good distance away from the bar. We were enjoying our glasses of scotch, discussing the market crash and the internet boom that everyone was obsessed about. "This was meant to happen", said Nate as he took a swig of his expensive scotch. He was a Harvard guy, who came from a rich family in Long Island. For him, becoming a lawyer was about status and reputation. He was smart but lacked the guts to do what it took to be the best. He was an entitled brat. There was constant, mostly unhealthy, competition between us associates at the firm, and I was the one they hated the most. For them, I was an outsider and the one who they felt the most threatened by.

Although New Yorkers considered themselves to be a sophisticated class of people, many of them were not far from being driven majorly by their primeval instincts. Like animals, they were governed by territorial parameters. Jealousy, competition, anger, lust and even rage surmounted the nerves of millions of people living in the city.

Our firm was no less than a glass cage - it held animals inside who were working tirelessly to tear each other apart in order to reach the top of the food chain.

The scotch and conversations were free flowing when Ben interrupted Nate and I and said, "Check out that girl at the bar."

"Which girl?" replied Nate as I sat there quietly.
Ben tried to discreetly point at the corner of the bar with his eyes, while articulating the words, "That blonde in the black dress".

She was sitting on a stool at the corner of the high table fixed at the bar. Nate and Ben were drooling over her, as were other men at the bar. She wasn't paying attention to anyone. She was on her own, ready to dismiss anybody who came her way.

I knew I had to get with her the moment I saw her. Not because of some connection I felt or a romantic idea I had in my mind but solely based on the feeling of competition and the want to enhance my ego by asserting my dominance over a territory where other men had tried and failed.

I stood up from the booth, and said to Nate and Ben, "See you guys at work."
"Where are you going?" They reverted in a drunken tone.
"Going home with that blonde." I replied with a smirk.
They laughed and said, "Not happening."
"That attitude is what separates you boys from me." I replied as I threw $50 cash on the table and walked away.

I strolled to the bar and sat down at the stool next to her. I ordered another glass of scotch, turned my neck to look in her direction and said, "You must be tired by now, having to reject all the men approaching you all night."

She laughed and asked, "are you another one of those men?"

I replied with a sentiment of pride in my voice, "I wouldn't let you buy me a drink, even if you insisted." And continued, "I know you are not interested in sleeping with someone for just a night. What you want is someone you can build a life with. Someone who sees you as more than just an object. Someone who sees you for your ambitions and dreams, your intelligence and depth. You want to be seen as more than just a pretty face. I am guessing you work in advertising."

"How did you know that I work in advertising?" she replied

with curiosity sparking in her crystal blue eyes.

"A calculated guess. If I am not wrong, you are here to remind yourself why you are better than others, why you don't want to settle for anything less than the top, and why you don't want to sleep with just any man. Because you know you deserve better. You are more precious than what they see you as." I continued.

Instead of facing the shiny liquor bottles behind the bar, we were now facing one another. She dropped her guard and looked directly into my eyes. Her frame was as if crafted delicately by a sculptor. The black dress molded into her lustrous skin in an exquisite delight. Her golden hair touched all the way till her middle back. Her lips sliced past the intensity of that moment, to simply engage with the light reflecting on our faces.

"What do you do?" she asked.
"I am a lawyer." I replied, and inquired, "what's your name?" while carrying my palm forward.
"I'm Veronica." She replied with a smile on her face, as our palms met.
"Nice to meet you, Veronica." I said with an affirmative tone in my voice and asked her, "so, what are you looking for in life?"
"A part of what you said and much more." She replied with authority in her voice.
"Why don't you tell me about it in detail over a glass of scotch at my apartment." I said as I looked directly into her eyes without any hesitation whatsoever.

There was a pause. Both of us were silent and looking into the other person's eyes. She waited for some seconds, to see if I would flinch my eyes or cave into the briefs of semantics. I didn't. And a few seconds later she said, "sure".
"Get your coat. Let's get out of here." I said to her.

It was the month of November, and it was cold outside. The greyness of the city, with its deeply embedded sirens of horror, was shimmering its way through the emptiness encompassing the soul-less towers of the city.

We left the bar to immediately get in a taxi and make our way back to my place, which wasn't far from where we were.

"Where do you live?" she asked me, as our bodies merged throughout that ride.
"I live close by. You will like it there." I replied.
"I really just came for a drink at the bar tonight." She said, as her eyes gazed into mine.
"I know you did. Me too." I replied. "Sometimes life has a funny way of working out."
I held her palms and didn't look away as she intensely stared into my eyes.

Moments floated away as we got back to my apartment. Veronica was sitting on the couch, admiring the buildings outside the glass windows. I was at the bar, preparing a drink for us.

"You seem like the kind of woman who probably enjoys a glass of scotch." I said from the bar, as she was looking out the windows.
"Yeah. I do." She replied.

I walked over to her with two glasses of scotch in my hand. I gradually sat down next to her, while handing over a glass to her.

"Thank you." she said, as her lips displaced seductively.

"You're welcome." I replied as our eyes locked.

"I can see you're very ambitious, just by looking into your eyes." I said. "Tell me more about yourself."

"I am from upstate NY but left my family as soon as I could. I have been living in the city for 10 years now. I know what it takes to start from nothing." She replied.

"Were you always in advertising?" I asked.

"I have done all kinds of jobs but for the last few years, I have been in advertising. It pays well. I am good at it. And this is where I see myself growing." She replied.

"What about you?" she asked.

"What about me?" I replied with a sly tone.

"You think you are the only one who can see through me. I see through the image you portray of yourself." She commented with a hint of ascendancy in her voice.

"Do you?" I replied with a sense of cynicism.

"I know why we are here. I am just a trophy for you. Something you can achieve to calm your nerves and fulfill your endless desire of being challenged." She stated.

"I would be lying if I said that's not true." I replied.

Veronica gently placed her drink on the table. She came close to me and whispered in my ear, "go on then, claim your trophy."

I hadn't met a woman like her before. She saw through me in ways no other woman had before. She was very much like me.

Our lips met for the first-time, seconds after she whispered in my ear, asking me to claim her for the night. We couldn't take our hands off one another. She submitted her body to mine, as we inhaled each other's senses throughout the tapestry of that night.

I knew she was different from the moment I first met her, and that one night of being with her eventually translated into us spending many nights together. She moved in with me six months later, and after living together for a few years, we eventually tied the knot to be legally pronounced as husband and wife.

I never really understood marriage or relationships but it is what society expects you to do as you go on with your life. It allows you to be valued, accepted and rewarded by the system that wants you to act the way that it does.

Both Veronica and I were plugged into a specific thinking sphere, to achieve the things we believed life was meant for. Together, we were a powerful force that had combined its resources and ambitions in the hunt to dominate the world of New York City.

My ambitions in life grew from my fear of ending up like my father. I wasn't striving for a life based on what was truly inside me, but based on what I thought would make me look good to the world outside. Like most people, I was guided by fear and therefore my ambition in life didn't originate from a space of inspiration.

In the process, I never really understood the force of ambition, which if risen from a place of purity and no ego, can manifest itself in a positive manner. But if risen from arrogance and greed, has the power to ruin everything in its path.

Veronica was on the same boat as me . She was a tigress, and an incredibly driven woman, which I found deeply attractive. But like me, she was also driven by fear. And although she destroyed all ideas of how women were supposed to be for me, there was always a part of her that was unhappy on the inside. Both of us were so blinded by our drive to become successful in the material world that we never questioned anything and never asked ourselves what it was that we truly wanted in life.

Years passed by hurriedly with the world around us only getting faster each day. Computers and cell phones started consuming our lives, and the world changed even more dramatically, with the invention of the iPhone just round the corner.

I was on my way to becoming a Partner at the law firm and Veronica was on her way to becoming the Creative Director at her advertising agency. It was in 2005 when we moved from my previous apartment, to a much bigger one in the Upper West Side. We had lived together for a few years by then, and I had just turned 34 when we decided to get married.

The new apartment was close to Central Park. It had an extra room, more space and everything we needed to impress others. We started collecting art works and antique pieces to decorate the apartment. They were souvenirs for when we had people over, which was plenty of times, as both Veronica and I knew the importance of knowing the right people in New York.

We were a team, working on our vision of creating an illusionary life of materialistic epitome, and neither of us could see beyond that vision. We didn't want children and were distant from our families. Veronica hadn't seen her parents since she had left their house. She never really talked to me about it. I didn't push her either.

I knew she didn't have a healthy upbringing. I knew that her father was an alcoholic and often physically abused her mother and her. She once told me that she had an older brother who went to the Army, but they never heard from him again.

"I can never go back to where I came from." She said to me one day, as we were sitting in our living room, having a drink. "Just the thought of it makes me sick."
"You don't have to." I replied.
"My father was a monster. I can never see that man again." She said. "I couldn't care less if he is dead already. I would like to burn the house he lived in, if I ever get the chance."
"What about your mother?" I asked.
"I don't know where she is. I think she ran away at some point. I don't blame her. I would have done the same thing, if I was married to that man." She replied.
"And did you ever hear from your brother?" I asked.
"No, nothing. I hope I get to meet him again." She said.

I hadn't seen my mother in a few years, even though she still lived in Queens. My brother Samir had left New York some years ago to go live in Oregon. I hadn't spoken to him since he left. He had sent me an email when he left.

> Dear James,
>
> I know we don't talk anymore, as you are busy with your life but I want you to know that I am moving away from New York. I could never fit in here. The busyness of it all would always get to me. I don't expect you to understand this.
>
> I am moving to Oregon. Hopefully, I can start a new life there and live in peace. I have always admired you for your willingness to chase after your desires. You were my hero growing up, and even though we have become distant with time, I have always loved you.
>
> I wish to see you again, and I hope we can be brothers again. If not, I accept your life choices and wish you well for everything in life.
>
> Take care,
> Samir

My mother didn't really like Veronica. The first time they met was for lunch in a fancy café in Tribeca, before Veronica and I got married. It was the time of fall. The weather was pleasant. We were seated outside the café in their open seating. I was wearing a suit and Veronica was wearing a white dress made of silk that touched her knees. Her shoulders were naked, and a silver pendant settled on her chest.

My mother arrived in her usual attire that she wore almost

daily to work. A long skirt that fell past her knees, along with a simple shirt that covered her neck and reached her palms. She was a simple woman, who lived her life every day with the grace of serving others.

I wasn't even close to being anything like her. Rather, I was becoming the opposite of her every passing day.

Veronica and I were sitting at our table when my mother arrived. She looked at me and then right away, looked at Veronica to say the words, "you're beautiful", with a shine in her green eyes. "Thank you", said Veronica, "it's so good to finally meet you. James has been talking about you for so long."

I hadn't been. I hadn't mentioned my family to Veronica at all. She didn't even know that I had an Indian heritage. I hid that fact from most people. Even when introducing myself, I would skip my middle name "Ahmed" and only use "James Walsh".

Nobody could guess that I was half Indian just by looking at me. I was aware of the biases that occupied people's minds in America based on family name and skin colour. So, I worked the system to my advantage. I knew what I had to do, and I did it without any guilt. I barely remembered my father anyway, so the little that I knew about India came from reading about it in books or through my mother, who was very fond of Indian food and was fascinated by its cultural history.

She used to tell Samir and I when we were young how she fell in love with our father.

"He was always so kind to me and I loved his cooking. All kinds of spices and the variety in the food. It was incredible!"

She never went into detail as to why they separated. She would always just tell us, "We come from different worlds – your father and I. And life is taking us on different paths." I do remember my father quarreling with my mother, not wanting to be separated. He didn't believe in divorce. Even though he had left India and his family, his conditionings from India were strong. At the same time, his soul couldn't be tamed in a domesticated setting. He struggled with the concept of being married. I think he was always fighting an internal battle between what he was supposed to do and what he actually wanted to do.

He tried his best to stay in our lives till the moment his body was dismantled by a car. The last memory I have of him was that of his burial. And with that, I had collected everything about him in an imaginary box and put it aside somewhere in my brain, so that I would never have to deal with it.

I denied everything about him. Although he never did anything wrong by me or my mother, it was easier to simply erase him to not feel the pain of his death. I became friends with numbness and that became my weapon to achieve whatever I wanted.

"So, Veronica, you're the first woman James has ever introduced me to." Said my mother in an elated tone.
"Really?" said Veronica and continued, "I'm not that surprised, Mrs. Walsh."

"It's Miss Walsh." My mother interrupted.

"Ohh sorry…. I didn't know. James hasn't told me many details about his family." Said Veronica.

"I was rather surprised when he told me that we were coming to meet you. But now that we are getting married, I wanted to meet you!" said Veronica in an ecstatic mode.

"Married?! You two are getting married?" My mother commented with her eyes stunned.

"Wait… James didn't tell you?" said Veronica, looking confused.

Both were now looking at me, as I sat there silently.

"Well… mom, we are getting married two weeks from today. And we would like to have you there."

"In two weeks?" My mother said in an irritated voice. "And you're telling me now?"

Veronica interrupted, "I'm so sorry, Miss Walsh. I had no idea James didn't tell you." She continued with sympathy in her tone, "we would love to have you there."

"Of course, I'll be there. I'm his mother." Said my mother in a dismissive tone. She continued as she looked at me. "James, you never tell me anything. Have you at least told your brother?"

"No, I haven't. He's not in New York anymore. He would anyway feel out of place with our guests. It's better this way." I declared.

There was sadness in my mother's eyes, but I was heartless

to even acknowledge it. I felt no guilt, nothing. The marriage was like a façade, anyway. It was less of a relationship based on the values of love and care, but more of a contract that fit the needs of both parties involved. It was an agreement between our minds, which wanted to live per the demands of a life we had both envisioned for ourselves. We had agreed to be in this contract for our selfish desires of what we wanted our lives to look like.

We expressed the phrase, "I love you" countless times, but never meant it. We were both disconnected from our hearts. We were lost in the madness of New York, disavowing ourselves in the process from feeling anything meaningful.

Veronica had hired wedding planners for the day. It was all organized in a spectacular fashion. We had our colleagues, clients, so called friends attend the wedding, which took place in a beautiful rooftop location in Upper West Side, overlooking the central park. Both Veronica and I weren't religious, so we just said our vows to one another.

I knew that not a single person who was present at that wedding, including Veronica, would take a bullet for me. The only person who would, my mother, left half an hour into the whole charade. She couldn't bear to see what I was becoming. I was totally lost in the madness of the stories I was busy creating, without even realizing what I was losing in the process.

CHAPTER THREE

NUMBING SENSATIONS

"I will love you forever, no matter what happens." I declared as Veronica and I looked at each other with glitter in our eyes, doing our best to play the roles we had taken on for the day.

A pastor was next to us, guiding us through our vows. Our guests were standing in the open space with their glasses of champagne, pretending to be mesmerized by the perfection of that evening. The high rises encompassed our view. Veronica was looking stunning in her white gown. She always knew how to make her dresses look both sensual and sophisticated at the same time.

"I will hold your hands till eternity", said Veronica, as we pronounced our vows one after the other. I knew exactly what her vows were going to be. She had hand-picked them from the internet, contemplating which would sound the best. She even picked most of mine, and we rehearsed the vows several times before the occasion. Nothing about those vows was spontaneous. It was all planned, with every detail considered, so that the event could leave our guests captivated.

We continued with our list of fabricated vows as the audience "awww-ed", almost in sync. I ended our stream of vows with, "everything that I am and own is yours. From this moment forward, I am yours, and you are mine." And then the pastor asked us if we accepted each other as husband and wife. We said, "I do" and kissed as if we were being recorded for the shoot of a film.

Our acting was brilliant. Nobody, including ourselves, could tell we were acting. We were so ingrained in our parts, that at some point we were just living them. We were conning ourselves through our bones. It was all about what the audiences thought of us. We were extremely shut off on the inside, unaware even of the distinction that existed between the outside and the inside.

The celebration went on all night. We had influential people from various industries attending our wedding. These kinds of events are the venue for a lot of networking. It was all about who worked where, and how they could profit from meeting the other person. We knew all this very well and made sure we got the right circle of people attending our wedding, so that we could benefit from the whole thing.

It is all about knowing the right people in New York. If you know the right people, it opens many doors for you. Both

Veronica and I had to kill our earlier identities and create new ones to infiltrate the exclusive circles of New York.

Being a woman in the world of advertising, Veronica played this game better than anyone I knew. She had mastered the art of deception and manipulation. She knew exactly what to say and what to do, to get people to believe in something, and act according to her will. Even I couldn't understand her intentions on many occasions. She was a master manipulator; and our entire relationship was a product of that. I prized it though. It is what I wanted. I wanted to be with someone who could play along with my aspirations of dominating the world of New York.

Nothing much changed in our lives post marriage. We had already been living together for a few years and were quite accustomed to the roles we were busy playing by then. We didn't fight much either. We didn't have the time to fight. Both of us were only getting busier in our individual lives, taking on more responsibilities at work, earning more income and then utilizing that income to buy more things to impress other people.

Sometimes we wouldn't see each other for weeks, even though we technically lived in the same place. Both of us worked 16–18 hour days. Our physical intimacy had faded with time, and we were severely blocked emotionally to even recognize how miserable we were.

Occasionally I would sleep with other women, and she with other men. We didn't have to tell each other about it. We knew that it was happening, but we didn't care. Our marriage was an image we had created to showcase the outside world. Whatever happened within didn't matter as long as it didn't affect our long-term vision of creating the life that we both desperately desired.

We always just pretended to love one another but never actually did. We had never loved even ourselves to be able to love the other person. We did care for one another though and would show up if the other person needed anything.

We thought of love as weakness. Emotions as distractions. Feelings as vulnerabilities that diverted us from our paths. We killed anything that made us look frail, without doubting or second guessing it for a second.

In 2007, the housing market of the USA collapsed, inciting a global recession and causing millions of people to lose their jobs overnight. It would be termed as the 'Great Recession' in the following years. The unemployment rates were strikingly high and many people we knew lost their jobs.

It was a few years into our marriage when this economic crisis unfolded. Veronica and I had been asked by our bosses to cut corners at work - i.e., not hire more people and fire the ones who were not essential to the company. As heartless executioners, that's exactly what we did, without any guilt. I had to fire some of the junior associates at the firm, to make sure I hit my quarterly profit targets.

The world of advertising was hit way worse than the world of law. Most companies had to cut down their advertising budgets following the recession, stirring a major loss among advertising firms. I had never seen Veronica this stressed before. She was losing weight and hair from the amount of stress she was taking at the time. In those days, she was going through packets of cigarettes faster than she could inhale oxygen.

It was late at night, when we were sitting in our living room indulging in a glass of scotch to switch off the mind, when she said to me, "James, what are we going to do?" sounding remorseful. "We shall ride the storm till it ends." I replied after swallowing the entire glass of scotch in one gulp. "We have worked so hard to create all of this. I don't want to lose it." cried Veronica in her drunken speech.

I had never seen her this vulnerable before. She could no longer hold herself.

"We came this far, didn't we?" I said, and continued, "We will continue to move forward."
"But what if there is no forward?" She inquired in her desperate tone.
"There is. Trust me." I commented, as I poured myself another drink.

It was the first time that I witnessed Veronica's insecurities surfacing. It was the first time I felt something for her. For a moment, we were more than our stories, and I felt intimately connected to her.

Veronica dozed off on the couch as I was overlooking the tall buildings outside our broad windows, while standing alone in the echoing silence of New York City. The grimness of the city had started flaring through my veins. Something within me was starting to shift. I was holding it all down, not acknowledging anything and creating new boxes within myself to keep on hiding through the face of it all.

The recession had incited anger and distrust amongst the American people for the government, banks and large corporations. Someone had to be blamed for the crisis that had left millions jobless and in a state of desperation. The government had stepped in to bail the large banks, who had filed for bankruptcy and put the blame on immigrants and poor people for having made bad economic decisions and therefore, causing the markets to collapse.

Greed, driven by ignorance and lack of accountability, had caused the economic system to bend on its knees.

I walked through Wall Street and saw hundreds of people exiting the buildings with their cardboard boxes after losing everything they had worked for. It was a different image from what I remembered from my childhood, when I used to idolize the life of these same men.

Sometimes, reality doesn't kick in until we see it manifest in front of our eyes. As I saw the world of capital being choked by the ignorance of our actions, I felt something in me for the first time. I realized that everything I had been working for could disappear in just a second.

I questioned the significance of the system that had been rewarding me in monetary terms for the first time in my life. Sparked by fear, I wondered, "what if I become one of these men?" I realised that it could just as easily be me, carrying all of my life's work in just a box.

If left without a job, with no foresight of the future, how would we afford the mortgage on our million-dollar apartment? or pay the heavy expenses of our luxurious lifestyle? I asked myself.

My survival instincts were being triggered. I felt nervous, not knowing what was going to happen.

The entire image that I was busy creating of myself for the last many years could fall apart anytime. 'What would matter then?' was the question I had no answer to.

The collapse of the external structures elicited the demolishment of my internal ones.

In that moment, standing there outside Wall Street, a shift happened in my consciousness. I suddenly entered a darkened space. I couldn't fight this shift, no matter how much I tried.

It was something similar to what used to happen to me when I was a kid. But this time, I didn't lose my consciousness. I was aware of the shift. The force of it was powerful. I was no longer standing on Wall Street. There were no people next to me in this dark void. Nothing made sense. I felt confused and vulnerable. I screamed in the hollowness of this empty space, only to fall and lose my consciousness.

The next thing I remembered was waking up in a dimmed alleyway somewhere in midtown. My body was hurting. I had bruises all over it. I lethargically got up to make my way to a bar and get a drink. I had no idea what had happened to me on Wall Street. I didn't know how I even got to midtown. My mind was blank. I walked into the first bar I could find, ordered a drink and with it, tried to forget everything.

Something changed in me following the months after this incident. I couldn't forget it no matter how hard I tried, or how much I drank to numb my mind. Seeing the world of capital collapse in front of my very eyes triggered my deepest insecurities and fears. The shadows of the subconscious were surfacing. I was losing my ability to control everything. The silence of that dark void kept looping through my senses. I wasn't sure what to make of my reality anymore. There were distortions in the story, and I couldn't function the way I did for the last many years.

Doubts on blindly following a set structure started sprouting in my mind. How could this be the only way? I would often find myself asking this question. I didn't feel clear in my head and wasn't sure about what really mattered in life.

I didn't have the same motivation as before. The day after we connected deeply for the first time, Veronica went back to living her lie. But I couldn't continue working with the same intentions as before, after being swarmed by an unknown calamity of changing realities.

The economy started to recover after 2008, and we got back in the hustle of creating the life we had envisioned. I was going to turn 36 soon, and there were talks about promoting me to a partner at the firm. Veronica was on her way to becoming the first woman CEO of her advertising agency.

Our dreams were starting to manifest themselves the year following the Great Recession. Veronica was thrilled. I had never seen her this happy before. I didn't know what I felt. I was becoming distant from the present reality. Something was pulling me away from it. I didn't have a hold of what was real and what was not. My perception of the world outside was being questioned and torn apart.

"This calls for a celebration." She yelled in an elated tone one night when we were sitting on our couch drinking our glasses of scotch.

"If you say so." I replied.

"Let's go to the most expensive restaurant in the city." She continued in a jubilant speech. "We did it, James!"

I silently sipped my scotch with a slight nod of my neck.

We had ridden past the storms to arrive at our destinations, but it didn't feel right. I had never felt more miserable in my life before. My throat felt numb from having nothing to express. My face had grey hair with wrinkles that made me look much older than I was. I was losing hair on my head, and I no longer had the same drive I used to have when I was 26.

I knew something was not right, but I was ignoring the signs my body was giving me. I had only met my mother twice in the last 5 years and hadn't spoken to my brother even once. I didn't even know if he was still alive or what was he doing in Oregon.

After that incident on Wall Street, I no longer knew where I wanted to go. Everything seemed grey and hopeless. People around me started to seem worthless. Our apartment felt like a cage, with our precious collections staring at me in horror. I would walk around the apartment through sleepless nights, not knowing what was happening to me.

All my achievements meant nothing in those moments. The degrees on the wall looked like certificates of mockery, that were holding me cooped in a prison of my own creation - a creation that I wanted to be a part of so desperately that I killed everything good about me in the process.

I felt absolutely nothing in my body. Nothing.

I used to take the train every morning to work. It was faster and more efficient than taking a taxi. The train full of men looked exactly like me - wearing our suits, hooked onto our phones, looking towards the dirty floor of the train, avoiding eye contact with one another, pretending to be someone we were not.

After getting off the train, I would walk several blocks to arrive at the building in which my office was located. I would buy a cup of coffee on the way, to get my brain wired and ready for the day's battles. Being a lawyer and working for the corporate world required me to be cutthroat every single day. My clients weren't always the best of what humanity had to offer, but they had money and that's what our firm was after. All we cared about was winning and raising our profits. That's all that I cared about as well till the recent developments in my life. Nothing used to be enough for me. I had always wanted more and more. But now, I couldn't seem to care less about anything.

I was being promoted to a partner in the firm, one of the youngest individuals to have achieved that label. But I wasn't sure if I even wanted it anymore.

I was starting to feel things. Mostly unpleasant things. Alcohol wasn't helping keep me numb anymore. Sometimes, I would be standing by the window in my office, absolutely zoned out while looking at the endless horizon of buildings that comprised my view. Everything felt like an illusion. It didn't seem real.

My boss, Adam, said to me days before I would officially be termed as a partner at the firm. "You did it kid. You beat me by a year to become a partner at the firm." He continued, "you deserve it. I knew you had the potential. You proved me right."

"Thank you for providing me with the opportunity to learn from you, Adam." I replied. I don't know why I said that. I didn't even mean it.

Adam was 52 by then. He had grey curls and an oval face that cultivated a taste of his wrinkling skin. His eyes were brown in colour and rested firmly behind his glasses. He had a strong presence and a thick skin when it came to negotiations. I had learnt a great deal from Adam, who had a colliding work ethic. I had never seen him miss even a single day of work, as I hadn't missed one either. Together, we had taken our firm to new heights, defying the barriers of our alleged potential.

He was the only one I had some amount of respect for in the firm, as no other partner gave as much as he did every day. By now, he was divorced twice. He had one son with his first wife. Adam eagerly pushed his son to become a lawyer, but he could never cope with the pressure of it and found himself escaping through life abusing any substance he could get his hands on. Now, his son was a recovering drug addict and had spent most of his early twenties in rehabs.

Adam never talked about his family. I never insisted, either. That's just not what we did. All we ever discussed was work and anything other than work was merely a distraction.

Our lives seemed to revolve around the tapestries of New York City, with no sight of anything other than the reality we were sucked into.

That world was becoming irrelevant to me with every passing moment. I couldn't contain the locked boxes inside my head. They were dispensing, leaving my consciousness adrift into vast spaces of emptiness. I would be sucked into distant realities on an occasional basis, where nothing would exist beyond my grievances. A far-reaching world, where the creations of my current world wouldn't hold any significance.

My physical intimacy with Veronica had tattered with time, and I couldn't even remember the last time we had had sex. I did, however, have sex with another woman a few nights ago. She worked at a concealed bar located at the corner of 6th avenue and W 13th street. There was a sense of aloofness about the bar. I went to it late at night, after work. I came across it as I had decided to walk my way up through the haunting streets of New York. It seemed like the perfect place, where I wouldn't run into anyone from my known circles. I could find a moment of quiet inside and not be thinking about anything. The bar was kind of empty and I was indulging my senses in the lucidity of scotch.

She was pouring me my third glass of scotch, as she asked me in her upbeat voice, "long day at work, huh?"
"Always." I replied.
"You're a banker?" she asked me in a detracting tone.

"Worse... Lawyer." I replied with slight cunningness.
She smiled and said, "well, at least you recognize it."
"I live with it every day." I commented.

She was a beautiful, young woman. She had dark brown hair, crystal blue eyes, smooth white skin that was almost too refreshing to look at. I knew she wasn't from New York. She was still too naïve and had a sense of life around her.

"Where are you from?" I asked her.
"Not from here." she replied in a delighted manner. "Just moved to New York a few months ago to pursue my dream of theater."
"You like pretending to be other people?" I asked in a sarcastic tone.
She laughed and said, "I do. There's a lot that goes into becoming an actor and New York is the place to be, for theater. I have already started auditioning for shows and it's exciting."
"You do have the face for it." I commented in a nonchalant manner.

She leered and asked me, "what's your name?"
"Does it matter?" I replied in a dismissing tone.
"Not if you don't want it to." She said, "I'm Jessica."

"Nice to meet you, Jessica." I said, and asked her, "How's New York treating you?"
"I love it! Everything about it is so stimulating. I feel like there's so much to do here. I am constantly meeting new people and learning plenty." She said in a hasty tone.
"Enjoy the feeling while it lasts." I commented as I drained

another glass of scotch.
"The owner of this bar has been quite generous to me as well. He has given me a room upstairs to stay in. I mean it's tiny. But I love it. It makes me want to do more, so that I can have a nicer place for myself." She continued.

"Where do you live?" she asked me.
"My apartment is on the Upper West Side, but I feel more at peace when I come to these discreet bars. They help me forget everything, if only for some time."

"Is this the scotch talking?" She commented. "Why do you want to forget everything?"
"When you have been doing what I have been doing for this long, you sometimes just want to wrap your head around a thick carpet and not listen to anything or anyone. Stand distant from the crowd and not be a part of it." I said.

She paused for a second and said to me, "I have to close the bar soon, but if you want, we can go upstairs to my place and have a drink there."

I took a moment and said, "you seem like a good girl. Why do you want to take me, a married man?"

"Are you actually married though?" she commented with honesty in her bones.

"On paper, yes. But nothing more. This ring on my finger is a reminder why marriages don't work." I replied. "You like sleeping with men older than you, don't you?" I commented.

She replied, "I don't care about someone's age. Age is just a number. I care more about the connection I feel with the other person." she said.

"Huh... and you feel connected to me?" I inquired.
"Yes. I do. I sense something between us. Don't you?", she said.
"I don't feel anything anymore." I commented.
"I think you underestimate yourself." She said with a firm voice.

"Here's the thing they don't tell you when you are younger. Life isn't a straight line. It goes through ups and downs and sometimes you get to the place that you always wanted to reach, only to realize that the place you have arrived at actually does nothing for you." I gulped my drink and continued. "You feel only empty inside. And your body seems as if a hollow creature is slowly being poisoned by a venomous snake, one that is creeping into your throat, curling around your body, fiercely breaking all your bones and preparing to swallow you."

"Wow… that came from nowhere." She said.
"Well, now it's the scotch talking." I declared.

I ended up going to her boxed room after. It could barely hold two people inside. I couldn't stop myself from being pulled towards her. I was able to let go of myself when I was with her. We had sex all night. The box on which the mattress was placed was mangled. So, it made a sound the entire time we were together. Her feisty spirit made me feel alive for a few moments as her form sank into mine. I felt freer inside that tiny, boxed room with her, than my fancy office or my museum-like apartment, with my so-called wife, who I didn't even feel like touching anymore.

It was a week after my promotion to partner when Veronica and I went for our dinner to celebrate our successes. She had already taken over as the CEO of her ad agency, and we rarely spent any time together.

A 12-course meal in a Michelin star restaurant was being served to us. Veronica was drinking her expensive red wine and looking glamorous in her new outfit which she got custom made for the night.

We were being served one meal at a time. Every plate was delicately crafted with attention to detail in showcasing a unique blend of flavours and ingredients that were prepared by one of the best chefs in the world. The kitchen was like a lab where the chefs would experiment day and night to invent new recipes and dishes that couldn't be replicated anywhere else in the world.

It wasn't considered one of the best restaurants in New York for no reason. Just to get a table for two people could take up to 6 months. We didn't have to wait for 6 months, however, because Veronica was friends with the owner. She had got the restaurant featured in top food magazines of the country. Most restaurant owners, event managers, PR people and journalists knew Veronica. She had become an influential figure in the world of advertising and media. Many young women looked up to her and men wanted to sleep with her. She had created her image to be one of a desirable woman, who knew how to get the most out of people by using her wit and charm.

I used to love this trait about her when we first met. But now, it made me feel imprisoned as I knew it was all just an image she had created of herself.

Every detail in that restaurant was crafted to perfection. The lighting, the aroma, the service, the aesthetics, they were all aligned to deliver a unique experience of culinary arts. It wasn't just food that was being served at the restaurant. It was an orgasm being delivered on a platter. The people sitting at the tables around us were the most influential people of New York.

I was feeling a sense of revulsion as I sat among a pretentious lot of people, who were absorbed by a superficial life, like mine, where everything about us was fake. Our entire appearance, be it our clothes, personality, way of talking, were simply the ingredients of a mindless consumer that we had become. I felt incarcerated sitting in that restaurant.

"This is one of the best restaurants in New York, James." She said to me, feeling aroused. "I am aware of that." I replied with a straight tone.

"Can you at least pretend to look happy?" said Veronica in

a demanding appeal. "It takes people 6 months to get a table here. I could get us a table here in a week with a single call." "Sure, I can pretend. Because that's all we do Veronica. We pretend. Our entire lives, that's all we have done." I replied. "And look where it has brought us. We are sitting in one of the finest restaurants of New York, having earned our spot in this city." She declared.

"Yes, we have. And look how miserable we are. Our marriage is a joke. The work we do means nothing to us. We can't even look in the mirror anymore and know who the fuck is standing there." I said in a high pitch.

"What are you talking about? What's been going on with you these days? This is what we always wanted." Cried Veronica.

"We did. But, why? Did we ever ask ourselves that?" I declared. "We did what we thought we were supposed to do. And now that we are here, it seems to me that we have lost the light within ourselves in the process."

"Why do you always have to spoil the mood?" asserted Veronica.

The servers, dressed in all white, were gracefully changing our plates, pretending to not hear the argument we were having. We were slowly gathering the attention of the people sitting at the tables next to us, judging us for our raised voices.

"This is not spoiling the mood, Veronica. This is stating the fact that we are two miserable people, living a miserable life, while pretending on the outside that everything is fine." I said.

I couldn't hold it any longer. It all started pouring out of my clogged veins. Veronica was stunned. Her brain couldn't fathom the words that were coming out of my mouth. She was so ingrained in her reality that these words were alien to her. They would have been alien to me also, several years ago.

But, by this point, I was simply having a nervous breakdown and could not hold it inside anymore. My insides were rotting, and it was as if a lightning was striking my heart, tingling my senses and making me feel numb.

Even though I did not know what, I knew something had to change. I couldn't continue going on this way. My insides were screaming at me, and I wanted to be screaming out in that hollow space, where my consciousness would dip in for a timeless frame.

The illusion of my reality was flouting, and I couldn't cope with the wreckage of it.

CHAPTER FOUR

CAGED BY A PRISON

Veronica and I no longer slept in the same room.

The distance between us was only increasing each day. We hadn't spoken since our feud at the fancy restaurant where with each course of that 12-course meal, a new layer of despair clung to my skin.

It was a confrontation based on years of baggage that I had been carrying. I couldn't think straight after that night. Veronica went back to living her normal life but for the first time in over a decade, I deliberately chose not to go to work. It wasn't a good impression on my part, as I had just been promoted to Partner, but I was starting to care less and less.

It was the summer of 2009. The iPhone had just released a few years earlier and the world was changing quickly with phones becoming smarter and humans becoming more dependent on gadgets. Technology was integrating into our lives and changing the way we worked and lived at an exponential pace.

I left my apartment on a Monday morning with no destination in mind. Instead of taking the elevator, I climbed down the 44 steps of stairs from my floor. It took me a while to get down, but I didn't mind as I was in no hurry to get anywhere.

I wasn't wearing a suit but a simple button-down shirt and pants. I passed by the front desk of my building, where David, the concierge, acknowledged my presence with a sense of astonishment in his eyes. "No work today?" he asked. "Not today, David." I said calmly, as I got out of the revolving glass door of our building and stood on the sidewalk outside.

I would always take a right out of that door, in a mindless fashion, to get to the subway station a few blocks away. But that day, I decided to take a left and wander. I had left my phone at home, along with the endless list of things that I had to do in the coming weeks.

I was observing the variety of stores, bars, restaurants and supermarkets as I walked from one block to another. The crowd of New York, just like always, was ever too busy to care for what was happening in the world outside. They were hurriedly passing by one another, getting on with their day's tasks.

At some point during the walk, I saw Central Park and moved in that direction. I entered the park and was soon near the reservoir in the middle of it with a gothic bridge nearing my sight. I kept on trailing across the park and eventually came out on the Upper East Side.

I remembered my interaction with Jessica, the waitress I met a few days back. Her comment about how there's so much to do and see in New York was true. Just on my walk, I had encountered musicians on the streets, performers in Central Park, and cultural events happening in trendy spots. I saw something new and interesting every minute. It was stimulating my mind, and I wondered why I had never done this before.

Soon I saw the esteemed Guggenheim Museum, designed by Frank Lloyd Wright. It was a treat for the eyes. I had never been inside the museum so, I bought a ticket to enter the museum and found myself wandering around the space in awe, exploring the different exhibitions on display.

Even though Veronica and I had collected many paintings in our apartment over the years, none were out of appreciation for the art or the artist. I didn't know how to do something without thinking how it would benefit me and my image in some way or the other. Veronica was the same. We were both consumed with protecting and growing our images, to a point where we had become prisoners to it. The only difference between us was that I was starting to realize the imprisonment of our illusionary lives, and Veronica was only going deeper into its cage.

Being alone with myself and exploring the city made me feel things. I had been so withdrawn from my emotions that I wasn't even aware whether there was any beating left in my heart, any capacity left to breathe and let go.

As I slowly moved from one exhibition to another, climbing up and down through the motionless stairs of the wonderfully crafted Guggenheim Museum, I came across an exhibition, documenting the photographer's travels across India.

Till this moment, I had rejected everything Indian. It was my defense mechanism to stay away from anything that could remind me of my father. I had never even been to an Indian restaurant, seen a Bollywood movie or heard a Hindi song. I was a white man, living in a reality fostered by white men with an outlook that made me forget my Indian roots and my father.

My feet were hesitating to step into that exhibition room. The blockages in my mind were stopping me, but I pushed through them and moved forward. Somewhere in my subconscious, I knew it was not a coincidence that I came across this exhibition. I couldn't keep hiding from my shadows. I had to face them.

I slowly walked into the exhibition. My body was trembling, as I was simultaneously entering a deep place in my mind, which had been masked for a long time.

The walls of the exhibition were draped in black, and photographs laminated in humongous frames hung on the walls. Lights were installed on the ceiling at an angle that reflected the photographs and made them come alive.

My eyes couldn't stop staring at the colorful images on display. One photo had a sadhu in orange tainted clothes, long dreaded hair, sitting on steps near a water body. A sunset was transpiring in the distance. The colors were unreal; New York seemed so grey and dark in comparison.

As I slowly walked through the exhibition, I saw another photo that caught my eye. It was an Indian woman dressed in a colorful saree, sitting on the floor. She had the most joyful smile on her face. As I kept looking at the photo, tears started falling down my face. I touched my face in surprise; I couldn't even remember what crying felt like. At that moment, it felt exhilarating. I didn't care what others around me would think. For the first time in my life, I felt a little alive -- that too by just looking at a photo. There was another one of a group of monks. Their faces looked so childlike and festive. There was one photo of young kids, from the slums of Mumbai, smiling while waving at the camera. Looking at them, I realized that I didn't know what joy felt like.

Hours went by as I stared at the photos in that exhibition. All those photos of India triggered something deep in me. I couldn't have enough of them. I was aware of the marketing element that went into showcasing those pictures in a manner that would incite such a response from the audience. But for me, it was more than that. A part of me that I had killed many years ago was rising from the grave and screaming at me, probing me to look at it.

I was shedding skin as tears dripped down my cheeks. I almost felt high from being in that exhibition. It had teleported me away from New York and into certain blind spots where all my stories about life had come to a pause. For a brief second, I could witness myself as an individual who stood detached from the stories and independent of all human creations.

A shift transpired in my consciousness, the one similar to what happened during the Wall Street incident. This time, I tried to stay as aware as I could through it. I was teleported to a darkened, formless space. I couldn't see anything, but I could hear some voices in the background. The voices sounded familiar but they weren't loud enough for me to figure out who they belonged to.

It was painful for my mind to concentrate on those voices. I felt nauseous. I was struggling to keep my awareness intact in this altered course of reality. The voices became louder and, so did the pain in my head. I couldn't hold it any longer. My consciousness drifted apart. I blacked out.

I wasn't sure how much time had passed when my eyes kindled. I was seated on the floor outside the exhibition. My back was resting on a wall. One museum staff member, a lanky man, was standing ahead of me asking repetitively, "are you ok? Are you ok? We have called for an ambulance. It will be ok."

"It's not necessary. I am fine." I said as I regained my consciousness. I quickly got up and walked away from the person. "Wait… wait…." He screamed.

I ignored his call and rushed out of the museum, confused and embarrassed.

It was dark by the time I exited the Guggenheim Museum. It took me a second to regain my senses. The streets were busy as usual. I took some deep breaths and walked a few blocks to get on a subway towards lower Manhattan. I decided to make my way to the bar where Jessica worked. It was a rather spontaneous call.

I hadn't seen her since the morning I left her apartment. She was still in bed, lying naked next to me. I woke up to dress myself, kissed her on the forehead as I said bye to her. She said, "you're leaving already?" in her sleepy voice.

"Yes. Got work to do. Take care of yourself." I said, as I walked a few steps to arrive at the door. "How do we meet again?" she inquired. "We don't", I replied indifferently as I left her apartment.

I don't know why I was going to that bar, but I just felt like seeing Jessica again. It wasn't something I had done before. My occasional one-night stands never meant anything. It was always a mutual understanding between two parties to solely be together for the pleasures of the flesh, without any expectation or promise of seeing each other again.

I got to the bar, which was slightly busy. I couldn't see Jessica. I asked the bartender, "you know the girl who works here? Jessica?" He replied in a straight tone, "yeah."
"Where is she?" I inquired. "It's her day off." He remarked.

I left the bar and went to her apartment upstairs. I climbed the narrow stairs to arrive at the floor above the bar and knocked on the wooden door. The door opened soon, and there she was.

"Well, this is a surprise." She said with a straight face.
"I am sorry if I am interrupting anything, but I didn't take you for breakfast that morning. Can I make it up to you?" I asked with a genuine spirit.
"I thought you didn't want to see me again." She replied.
"It's more complicated than that. I am only starting to find out. Hear me out?" I said with a cry in my voice.

She paused for a second. Maybe it was the desperation on my face or the plea in my voice that made her say, "Ok. I'll hear you out."
"Great. Are you hungry? We could get dinner." I said.
"Now?" she replied in a hasty tone.
"Yeah! I saw a diner across the street. It looks nice." I said

with a smirk on my face.
"I could eat something, and that diner has good food." She replied with a smile.
"Let's do it then." I commented.

We left her apartment and walked across the street. We sat on a booth with leather sofas fixed to the glass windows. We could watch people walking by on the sidewalks from our seat.

"I love the food in diners." I commented.
"Me too. You're not wearing your suit today?" she inquired.

The waitress at the diner interrupted to inquire about our order. We ordered two plates of their special - hash benedict.

"I owed you breakfast." I said to Jessica.

She smiled, took a pause, and asked, "So, what's going on with you? You seem different today."

"I took a day off work today. Walked through Central Park. Went to a museum. Saw an exhibition that shook some things in me. And then I felt like seeing you, so I came here." I replied.

"Hmmm…" she said, and continued, "what was the exhibition about?"

"It was the work of a New York based photographer, Tania Groom. She had documented her travels in India. It was pretty special." I said with a certain gravity in my voice.

"India? Huh!" Jessica replied, "That must have been a colorful exhibition."
"It was and was deeply personal at the same time." I remarked.

"Why personal?" She asked.
"I don't share this with many people, but I am half Indian." I said with slight hesitation.

"Really?" She looked surprised, and continued, "I couldn't tell. You don't look Indian. This is so cool! Why don't you share this with people? It's very interesting."

"I have only recently started asking the 'whys' of life. Till now, I had been living in a set mindset. Anything outside of that mindset was out of question for me." I declared.

"This is good." She said, "We should always be open to life." She finished with a smile.
"You're very wise for your age." I joked with a sense of truth in it.
"How old do you think I am?" She asked in an inquisitive tone.
"I don't know. You tell me." I replied.
"I am 24." she said with confidence, "and you?"
"I am 12 years older than you. But I feel like you have figured out life more than I have. So, you're much older than me in many ways." I stated.

"I think we are all on our own little journeys. I like to be inspired in life. That's why I couldn't live in Virginia anymore. It's where I was born, but not where I belong. I needed a change." She declared.

As the night progressed, I found myself sharing things with Jessica that I hadn't even said out loud to myself. It was kind of bizarre but healing at the same time. I wasn't pretending to impress her or say things to get something out of her. Neither was she. It felt natural and right. I hadn't experienced that before.

The hash benedict was delicious. I was eating with no remorse and just enjoying the food.

"Somebody's hungry." Commented Jessica with a slight sass.
"I was famished. The food is so delicious. I haven't enjoyed a good meal in a while." I replied with heightened spirits.
"Don't let me hold you back." She said, as she continued, "how's your wife?"

"I have no idea. We haven't spoken in a few days. I haven't even seen her, for that matter." I replied, sounding casual.

"Is she traveling? You don't even see her when you go to sleep?" She inquired.
"We haven't been sleeping in the same room. And she is swamped at work with lots of responsibilities, so she rarely has any time." I commented.

"What about you? Aren't you busy as well?" She asked.

"Yeah… kind of… I became a partner at my firm. It is the position I've always wanted. And now that I have it, I don't really want it…. I don't know what I want." I said with honesty in my voice.

"I think it's ok not knowing what you want, isn't it?" Jessica said. "Have you ever thought about doing anything other than practicing law?"

"I haven't really tried many things in life. I don't come from much, and to get to where I am, I had to have a single-minded focus." I said

"Do you like being a lawyer?" she asked.
"I don't know if I like being a lawyer, but I am definitely very good at being one." I replied.

"You can be good at something and not like it at all." Jessica noted, "Do you think you are happy in life?"

I took a breather and replied, "that's a question no one has asked me before. The answer would be a definite NO. I don't even know who I am anymore. I have only recently started to feel things. Today, I cried at the museum. It was the first time I have cried since I was a kid."

Her blue eyes were beholding my brownish-green eyes with empathy and kindness. I felt human again.

"Why did you agree to sit with me, even after the way I treated you that morning?" I asked.

"I believe in giving people second chances. And I knew that it wasn't easy for you to come down here and do what you did today." She replied with a forgiving tone.
"It's the first time I have done something like this. And it feels good to be nice, for a change." I said.

"I think there's more to you than you realize. Big changes are coming for you, James." Jessica declared as she delivered that message through her eyes.

I stayed silent as I let that sink in. She was still looking into my eyes, not expecting anything in return. I couldn't digest the fact that she was only 24 years old. She was so wise and accepting, without forcing it. She was seeing me beyond the image that I portrayed for the world outside. My mind felt at ease in her company.

"Do you want to go for a walk?" She asked me, once we finished our meals. I agreed without reluctance.

We left the diner with our bellies full. I was following her lead, as we strolled past West Village and made our way towards midtown.

"I love mindlessly walking through New York. It energizes me", commented Jessica, as we walked in a slow pace from one block to another. "You come across the most random things in this city."

During our walk, she pointed out so many places and things that I had never noticed before. A fact about a building, or a story pertaining to some old theater that we passed on our way. She had this naïve sense of curiosity, which was almost childlike. She was very cultured and loved art, not to pretend or glamourize it in the eyes of other people, but simply because she loved it.

I could tell by her genuine nature that she really cared about the things she talked about. She was passionate about being an actor and working in theater. She wasn't just pursuing it for fame, but sincerely appreciated the art form.

"People like you are rare to come across in New York." I said to her.
She smiled and rejected my comment with this naïve hopefulness, "you'll be surprised, James. There are good people everywhere."
I laughed, with my cynic hat on, and said, "Not in New York."

She acknowledged my comment and replied with a cliché statement that one would find in a self-help book, "life is what we make of it. It's on us to decide what we want to bring to this world."

"You really are a rare one." I said, and continued, "I hope New York doesn't kill this spirit of yours."
"Did it kill yours?" She asked.

"Honestly, I don't think I ever had it. And now, I feel like I am already dead inside" I replied with a stern face.

"I don't see a dead man walking. I see a man with a lot of potential, who is willing to give life another chance." Said Jessica.

"I see your point. But I am stuck in this endless loop where I've got bills to pay, and multiple responsibilities to take care of. I don't know what to do, and even if I did, I don't know where to start, or how!" I cried as I kept pouring my thoughts out in the open.

"There will always be things we have to do or take care of, but I do think there is value in trying, even if it's a tiny step each day." She continued, "And from what you have told me today, I feel like you are already facing things about yourself that you never did before."

I looked at her as she said that to me, and replied after a pause, "I have never been able to open up to somebody like this. That too, so quickly."
She smiled and said, "I am glad I could be here for that."

We nestled our way through the streets of New York, until we parted ways. She kissed my cheeks and said, "I had a great time tonight. Thank you for coming by to see me. I hope to see you soon." I nodded my head in agreement and let my feet lug me back to my apartment.

It felt like days had gone by since I had been in my apartment. I went to bed with a smile on my face, my heart feeling a little lighter. I didn't bother Veronica, but I knew it was time to have a conversation with her about separating. I no longer wanted the same things as her. I didn't know what I wanted in life; but the least I could do was start working on removing the things I knew I didn't want. If there was still hope for me, I wanted to pursue it. I wasn't ready to give up on myself. I knew that it wasn't going to be easy, both for me and Veronica, but then again, what is life without some obstacles.

I wasn't happy. I wasn't in love with Veronica. I wasn't in love with my work. I had lost the passion I had for it. I didn't like the people I called friends. I despised most of the stuff we had in our apartment. There was no meaning, no purpose, no sense of excitement in my days. Money had shackled me more than it had freed me. The drive of childhood, from wanting to escape that life in Queens had brought me to a junction where I felt stuck and clueless of what I was doing.

My past was starting to haunt me. Things I had suppressed and never dealt with were ravaging in the form of a cocktail that was ceaselessly swirling inside my head and my heart. It was all happening at once. Flashes of my forgotten childhood would film behind my sealed eyes. I sometimes saw my father in those flashes. His presence in those memories felt like a coded message, which I couldn't make sense of.

Deep shifts were transpiring in me, and I didn't know what to do with them. I felt anxious and breathless most of the time. I would smoke cigarettes to help me breathe and feel at ease, but the jitters in my body were constant. My mind was foggy, and I couldn't focus. The ghosts of my childhood were ravaging me every second.

CHAPTER FIVE

A LAWYER'S JUDGEMENT

I woke up the next morning and got back to the usual grind. I was in my new office by 9am. The words, James Walsh, were painted on the glass door that catered to a bigger space and grander view of the city. I, however, felt sick inside.

Adam walked in moments later to congratulate me. "Took a day off to celebrate your success?" He remarked with a smile on his face.

"No celebration, Adam. Just had a day for myself to not think about anything." I said.
"Hmmm...." He whispered. "What is going to be your first step as a partner? I suggest you start building a team of competent associates."
I nodded in agreement, even though that's not what I wanted to do.

"I'll leave you to it then." Adam commented as he began to make his way out the door.

"Do you ever wonder what would happen to us, if we were not lawyers? Not part of this game? If we were not pursuing the things that we are at the moment." I asked Adam just as he was about to exit the door.

He turned around, took a slight pause and replied with a smirk on his face with a hint of arrogance in his voice, "our clients would desperately be in need of good lawyers then."

"Fuck the clients, Adam. They don't care about us. They only care about the work we do. We are easily replaceable. As long as they get their way and more money in their pockets, they keep us around. We will mean nothing to them if we are unable to deliver." I declared with a frustrated tone.

"And that's why we always deliver and work hard to be good at what we do. Hence, they are forced to keep us around." Adam said to me with aggression in his eyes.
"That's not the point I am trying to make." I said.
"What's your point?" He asked.

"Never mind". I replied.
He knew I was holding something inside. So, he insisted that I speak openly.
"What's the matter kid?" He asked.

"Doesn't it sometimes feel meaningless to you? We are solely working for money, representing people who don't give two shits about anyone but themselves." I said.

"You don't get to rise through the ranks in New York by thinking about other people. We are not a charity. We are lawyers and we get paid for being competent and ruthless." Adam asserted.

"I am aware of that, Adam. But, don't you think there's more to life than that? Look at all these people sitting outside. Don't they look miserable to you? And look at us, there's no sense of life left in us." I noted as I got up from my chair and pointed at all the people sitting in their cubicles outside.

"What are you talking about? This is what we do. This is who we are. This is how the world works. You don't get to be where we are, without losing sleep at night and hair from your head. Life takes everything from us, and this is our only chance of taking things back." Adam commented. "We are not miserable. We are lawyers in New York. We have to be cut throat as we go on to define our legacies."

"What legacy are you talking about, Adam? Your son is a drug addict. Your first marriage didn't work out. And your second marriage isn't going that well either." I said, with discontent in my voice. I couldn't believe what I had said in my anger. I wanted to take it back, but at the same time, I did not. While it was the truth, no matter how harsh, I knew I had crossed a line.

Adam was taken aback for a moment, but then he fired at me with his wounds surfacing. "You know nothing about my son or my marriage. They have nothing to do with what we do here", he started in an angry tone.

"Don't they? They have everything to do with what we do here. My marriage is also a joke. I don't even know who Veronica is. I don't think she knows me either. All the stuff that we have amassed over the years, these possessions and titles, feel more like a burden to me than anything else." I replied as I swayed my palms to point at the buildings outside. "They own us, Adam. We don't own them. They keep us in check, in line; so that we function in order and live according to the boxes of black and white. Nothing more. Nothing less."

"I get it, James. It's hard when your marriage is falling apart. I have been there. I see where all of this is coming from. Don't let what's happening in your personal life distract you from the work we do here." Adam said with a hint of empathy in his voice.

"This isn't because my marriage is falling apart. My life with Veronica was more a deception than anything else. It was meant to be broken. I am glad it's happening now rather than later. But the point I am trying to make here is beyond marriage. It is beyond everything. We are living our lives trapped in these boxes of black and white, functioning as highly efficient robots, controlled by money, fame and power. We are not living as humans." I cried out.

"I see where you are coming from. But we are effective lawyers. It's our job to find loopholes between the black and white. And that's what makes us good at what we do. Without these boxes, there wouldn't be any room for the work that we do." Adam declared.

"But is that all there is to us? We are just swinging between these boxes, fulfilling our duties and responsibilities for the clients, for the superficial life that we have built in this city, with so-called friends whom we can't even trust and open up to, because we are afraid of being judged." I remarked.

"We have no choice, James. This is how the world works and if you want to make something out of yourself in this world, you have to play by its rules to win or get eaten by the sharks." Adam declared.

"I am done playing by the rules of this world." I declared with my body trembling.
"What do you mean you are done?" He asked in a rhetorical tone.

"It means that I am done. I can't do this anymore. I can't pretend everything is ok, when it clearly is not. I can't keep on living this lie. I no longer feel anything. I don't know who I am. I am miserable inside." I cried with my body shaking.

"We are not supposed to feel anything. We are lawyers. Feelings and emotions divert us from thinking logically and acting professionally. We need to keep our feelings aside and carry out the tasks that others aren't willing to do. That's what makes us good at our jobs." Adam noted.

"And what if this job no longer exists one day? What will

happen then?" I said. "Remember the crash? It could have been you or me, walking out of those buildings."

"These things happen, James. People like us will always find something else that we are bloody good at and make money while doing it." He replied in a casual tone.

"This can't be the only answer." I said in a rejected voice.

"Do you have other ideas?" Adam asked in a cynical tone.

I felt a deep current rising through my belly, and into my heart. I was looking outside the glass windows. The buildings outside the windows were, as if, staring back at me.

I took a deep breath to calm my nerves. Words rose through my heart, before I could stop them, "I am leaving Adam. I can no longer pursue this path. I know there's more to life than this, and I want to give it a chance."

Adam knew in that moment that I was serious, and it was beyond him to convince me otherwise. There was silence in the space between us.

"Good luck, kid. It's been a good run." He said and exited the office, sighing dejectedly as he went.

I stood in silence. Tears came to my eyes as the images of my past began to crumble. I felt vulnerable and open to the world as my life stood beyond the creations of humanity.

Life was finally taking its natural course, guiding me along towards a ride that I was yet to witness. I was willing to give it a chance and see what the unknown held in store for me .

.....

I left the office building in a state of solace. My eyes were misty. I didn't care about finding a box to keep my stuff in; I didn't care what they did with it either. "I hope they burn it", I thought to myself as I took off my jacket and tie and threw them in the garbage bin on my way out of the building. I felt like screaming and crying at the same time.

As soon as my feet hit the sidewalk, I began running to keep up with my overwhelming emotions. I ran without holding myself back, not worrying about what anyone around me would think of me. I kept running till I arrived outside Jessica's building. It was daytime and the bar was closed. I wasn't sure if she was going to be home, but I ran up to her place anyway.

I knocked on the door in a hurried manner, out of breath and sweaty. She opened the door and said with a stunned face, "You are making a habit out of this? Huh?"

I spoke with fragmented words, while trying to catch my breath, "I.... want to... tell you something..."
"I can see that!" she said in a humorous tone, "why are you all sweaty? And...like this?"
"I... just ran up here... from... Wall Street." I said while trying to get a hold of my breath.
"All the way from Wall Street?" her eyes widened, and her

pitch got higher.
"Yes.... I just quit my job." I stated.
"What? I thought you got promoted recently." Her eyes were still enlarged.

"Yeah. I was. It's something I had been chasing all my life but it just didn't feel right anymore. None of it did. I haven't felt this alive before." I remarked with a touch of jubilance in my voice.

"What are you going to do now?" She asked with a gentle smile surfacing on her face.

"For the first time in my life, I have no idea what I am going to do. I didn't plan on quitting my job today. I went to the office following my usual routine and I sat in my new office as a partner, almost ready to start my day even though I did not feel any joy. When my ex-boss walked in to congratulate me, I just couldn't hold it anymore. I exploded like a volcano that had been inactive for thousands of years. I had no control over it." I replied.

She kept smiling as I was shedding my layers at her mercy. She asked me in a gentle tone, "Do you want to get a cup of coffee at the diner across the street?"
"Absolutely!" I said.
"Wait for me downstairs. I will get changed and meet you in a few minutes." She whispered.
"Sure." I said and made my way down the stairs and stood along the sidewalk, looking up at the sky.

The sky was blue. It was daytime. Life was going on as usual for everyone around me. My excitement was slowly giving way to nervousness, as I had no idea what I was going to do next in life. I hadn't even thought about what Veronica was going to say. She is going to freak the fuck out, I thought out loud, and then laughed about it, because I really didn't care anymore.

This wasn't like me at all. I didn't know who I was turning into. A part of me that I had never experienced before was surfacing from the depths of my subconscious. I was witnessing myself and the world in a new light.

"Does Jessica have something to do with this?" I asked myself. "Things really started to change since I met her. Maybe she has a role to play!" I wondered.

I was having indescribable visions as I stood on the sidewalk waiting for Jessica. My consciousness was juggling between parallel realities. I didn't want to lose my consciousness, so I focused my attention on the thought of Jessica.

I thought about how Jessica and I had only slept together once and this was my third time seeing her after that. The last time we met was the most refreshing encounter I'd ever had with a woman. I could open up with her, speak without any guards and simply be in her presence. And even today, the first person I could think of as soon as I left the prison that I used to call my office was her. I knew she would understand what I was going through.

There was comfort in being with her. She wasn't the kind of woman I usually slept with. She was different; very centered and secure in herself. She didn't care what other people thought of her and was kind and fearless. She didn't feel like a real person at times. Maybe she was just an imagination created by my longing mind.

It was unimaginable to come across someone like her in New York. And for some reason, from the moment she entered my life, things had stopped going the way they were supposed to. The plans were becoming inconsequential by the minute.

She was acting as a reminder that I could be in a state beyond misery; that it was possible for me to feel things again and connect with a part of myself that had died somewhere in the process of becoming the person I had become.

I was breathing intently, releasing all the weight I had been carrying on my shoulders for so long. I was trying to be mindful of my breath in that moment. Soon, Jessica, with her soothing presence and glowing face, appeared before me and asked, "ready for our coffee?"

I was trying to get a hold of myself.

"Are you okay, James?" Jessica asked, as she gently placed her palm on my shoulder.
I exhaled a big chunk of air out of my mouth, and said, "Something is changing in me intently. I feel overwhelmed by it at times."
"I understand." She said. "Stay still and keep breathing."

I nodded in agreement. We stood there for some moments while I kept breathing. When I felt a bit better, we walked over to the diner across the street to sit at the same booth that we sat in the last time. The waitress, a middle-aged woman with red hair and a bright smile, walked over to our table and asked us, "what can I get you guys?"
"A cup of coffee for both of us would do." Jessica replied.
"Anything else?" she inquired.
"Nothing for now. Thank you!" said Jessica in a polite manner.

I was gazing out the windows while Jessica was speaking to the waitress. I had no idea what was happening to me. There was silence for a few moments before Jessica asked me, "How are you feeling James?"

Nobody had asked me that question with the intention of actually wanting to hear the answer to it.

"I don't fully know yet. Can't put words to the overpowering drive of sensations rising up my mind and heart." I expressed.

"Every time I see you, you look a little bit different." Jessica stated.
"Different how?" I asked.

"It's mostly your eyes… and the face. They seem to be letting go of things." Jessica shared.
"Hmmm." I murmured, not knowing what else to say.

"You're brave for doing what you did." Jessica said.

"I don't think there's anything brave about it. I just couldn't take it anymore. My body was giving up on me. I had started feeling dead inside, with no sense of hope or light. Everything had just become frustrating. I was annoyed by little things and people in general seemed more like a burden than anything else." I remarked.

"Life can seem like a burden sometimes, but we have to remind ourselves to not let our burdens become our baggage and stop us from living the way we truly want to." Jessica declared in her poetic voice.

"You're the weirdest 24-year-old I have ever met. How are you so wise at such a young age? You are like Yoda!" I said with humour and honesty.

She laughed and replied, "I don't know about that. I just think it's important to cherish life. To feel inspired. To share it with others. To learn from others and most importantly, to strive for the things we love doing."

"I wish I understood this when I was 24. Wouldn't have wasted so many years of my life doing the shit that I have been doing." I cried.

"I wouldn't call it a waste. I don't think anything is a waste. I think we are all on our individual journeys, going through unique things. I don't think we should judge ourselves for it. Rather, we should embrace the part of us that is constantly changing and can at any moment, take us on a completely different tangent. I think the key is in staying open to life." Jessica stated in a calm voice.

"I want to be more open to life now." I declared as we were sipping our freshly brewed coffees.

"That's the way to be! If we close ourselves from what life can offer, we limit our experiences in the little time that we have in this body." Commented Jessica with inspiration flowing through her eyes.

"I don't know where to start, or what to do now. It's nerve wracking, but kind of exciting at the same time." I noted.

"It's really exciting!" she said. "I am curious to see what's in store for you. I think you are going to face some tough internal battles, but you are going to come out of them stronger."

"There's definitely a lot to take care of now. I need to speak with Veronica and be honest with her. It's time for her and I to separate. We have deviated from our paths. I don't know my vision for life anymore, but it sure as hell doesn't align with hers. It's not going to be easy, but this is what I need to do." I declared with sadness in my voice.

"Yes. I understand. Even the thought of separating with your partner- a person you have been living with for so many years- can seem terrifying. But sometimes, we have to do what is necessary to discover our life's calling." She said, "It can be tormenting at first but that's just how life works. It constantly throws these steam rollers our way that force us to re-evaluate our choices and make decisions that may alter the course of our lives."

"That's some deep shit man…" I said, while inhaling a huge breath. "Everything you just said makes so much sense. I wouldn't have taken you seriously a few years ago, but at this moment, this is what I needed to hear." I continued. "You're not going to charge me for these words, are you?" I joked.

She laughed and said, "You have a good heart, James. I sensed it the first time I met you. You are just starting to realize it."
"You sensed it? How can you do that? I can't even feel my own heart." I said in a confused tone.

"I am good at reading people. Always have been as a child. It's something that comes naturally to me." Jessica said. "Growing up in Virginia, people always found me weird. I would somehow just know things about people, even people who were strangers. For a long time, I thought there was something wrong with me, until I realized that it was something I was born with. I was naturally intuitive, and when I embraced it as a gift, I was able to be true to myself and live a more authentic life."

"Hmm… what makes you sure that it's not just your mind playing tricks with you?" I asked.
"Because it doesn't come from the mind. It's difficult to explain. It's a very intuitive thing. I'm very sensitive that way." She remarked with clarity in her eyes.

"Ah, intuition, huh? That's something I am so distant from. I can't see beyond logic. Everything is analytical for me. I have been stuck in the mind for so long. I can't see beyond it." I said with a sense of frustration in my tone.

"Not anymore, James. I can see you getting out of the boxes you have built for yourself and getting in touch with your intuition. Our intuition is very powerful. It helps us connect with what we truly want, and once we are connected to it, we feel clear in ourselves." Jessica shared.

"Do you feel clear about who you are? Do you really want to work in theater?" I asked.

"Yes. I am clear. There's always more to come and we are constantly growing, but I certainly want to work in theater. It became clear to me when I was living in Virginia. I come from a small town, where I worked as a drama teacher for children in middle school. I loved everything about it." She told me. "Since I was a kid, I've loved acting and I was always active in theater work. But Virginia isn't where I could grow as an artist and meet people from around the world. Coming to New York was my dream. And now that I am here, pursuing what I love, even though I barely make a living, I still feel free in so many ways. I couldn't connect with people over there. I saw things differently and I wanted to evolve. I didn't want to limit myself. Change is good. Necessary even, for us to constantly challenge ourselves into discovering what we are capable of."

The honesty in her eyes, and hope in her words, were drawing me closer to a place within myself that had been untouched.

"There's courage in you, that is rare to witness in people these days. Most of us are constantly living in fear, struck by our insecurities and doubts. We numb ourselves to stop feeling things. We kill the life in us as we go on with our days with no sense of joy in what we do. Our souls become corrupt, minds corroded, and hearts non-existent. We lose everything human about ourselves in the process." I declared. "Look at me Jessica. I am empty inside. I don't feel love or inspiration. Not a single person would care if I died today. Nobody would even notice. Only my mother, if she ever found out, might come for the funeral. My life means nothing outside the cage that I have built. Even though I am worth a lot in the capital world, I feel worthless. Inside, I am fucking dead." I wept my heart out.

There was a pause. Her eyes were studying mine.

"I don't see a dead man. I see a man with a lot of potential, who is willing to give life another chance. Who is already taking action to bring himself out of his mind's prison. Who has a good heart and is capable of expressing his honest self." Jessica stated, as her words drilled through my chest.

A few drops of tears dripped down my eyes. I had never cried in front of a woman before. I considered it weak. But for some reason, I simply couldn't control myself anymore. Even though I was trying to resist, I just couldn't physically hold on.

“Let them flow. Let it all go. It’s ok. James.” She commented in an empathetic tone. “There’s no need for you to hold back anymore.”

The truth of that moment was gripping my eyes to break the stones concealed in my heart. The sorrows of the past were dialling into my organs. To wake me up. To let me simmer with the rising moments and be one with the oscillating frames of a heartless era.

CHAPTER SIX

BREAKING AWAY

"I am sure I will see you soon." Jessica said to me as we parted ways on the sidewalk outside the diner. She had to work at the bar in a few hours and I had to confront Veronica. It was time to have a serious and honest conversation with her. There was no delaying it anymore.

I walked all the way back to my apartment from the diner. My head kept playing various scenarios of how my conversation with Veronica could go totally erroneous. I was nervous and shaky. It wasn't something I had felt before; probably because I had never come face to face with things that truly mattered in life. Till now, everything had been a part of a typical sequence. Slowly breaking out of that was causing a lot of pain. My heart and mind had to work extra hard to be able to stand alone without conforming to the standard ideologies people adhered to.

It was late at night by the time I reached the apartment. I wasn't sure if Veronica was there, but I was really hoping she would be as there was a sense of urgency in me.

She was sitting on the couch, drinking a glass of scotch and smoking a cigarette. She was looking out the windows, captivated by the lights shining out of the multitude of buildings. She acknowledged my presence with a blink of her lashes as I quietly walked in.

"Haven't seen you in a while." She remarked as she inhaled a drag of her cigarette.
"Well... you have been busy with your world and I… have been taken hostage by mine." I replied.

She took a sip of her scotch, and shared one of her fantasies, "It would be nice to get a penthouse in the coming years. More space would be ideal. This apartment can feel cramped sometimes."

"More space for what? This apartment is more than enough for two people." I declared.
"Most CEOs have a place bigger than ours, James. And now, with me being a CEO and you a partner, we need to live up to that image." She remarked.

I took a deep breath and said, "Yeah…. About that…. I quit my job today."

Veronica's eyes got comically wide. She kept her drink on the table, moved forward and said with frustration in her eyes, "What?! What do you mean you quit your job? You can't quit. You just became a partner. This is what you have been working towards, for the last so many years."

"But it is not something I really want anymore, Veronica." I said in a gradual tone.

"I don't understand. How can you quit something moments after you got it?" She commented. "When did you quit? And why did you not ask me before doing such a stupid thing."

"Because for once in my life, I don't want to do what you or others want me to do. I am sick of this life. I am sick of us. We are two miserable people living a miserable life. Nothing feels good about our lives. We can't even talk to one another without pretending to be someone we are not. There's no love between us. I don't even remember the last time I touched you or the last time we were intimate. We rarely even see each other, and when we do, we either avoid each other or argue. I can't do this anymore." I yelled out to the ceiling.

Veronica stood up in anger and said, "You can't do this anymore? I am the one trying to get us everything in life. We are living in one of the best neighborhoods in the greatest city in the entire world. After all this, instead of feeling gratitude, you are blaming me for your inability to live up to the standards I have."

"I am not blaming anyone, Veronica. I am simply pointing out the fact that whatever we have isn't working for me anymore. I don't think it's your fault or mine. I just think we are moving in different directions in life. I don't aspire for the things I used to anymore." I replied in a mellow tone.

"What? You just changed overnight?" Veronica inquired, her volume increasing with every sentence.

"No. This didn't happen overnight. It is after years of hiding from a part of myself, which has now surfaced to overpower me. It is shedding light on things that I was running away from, all my life." I replied with a genuine call in my voice.

"What part? What are you talking about?" Veronica asked, looking more confused than angry now.

"It's difficult to explain. It's something I am going through at the moment, and I need a break from all of this to understand it better." I replied, "I do care about you, Veronica. We were nothing more than partners working to build a life that we both desired but I don't want the same life anymore. I know that you won't give up on the path that you are on. But it's not something I can be a part of."

"So, that's it - you are just going to quit? You are done? All these years of hard work would be in vain." She yelled. "You could have told me this was going to happen at the beginning. I wouldn't have wasted all these years on you."

"I didn't know this was going to happen. I didn't plan this out.

Here's the truth - we were never in love. We never actually got to know one another deeply. It was convenient more than anything else. We fit well on paper. The boxes ticked." I replied, "Take a moment and genuinely ask yourself Veronica, are you happy with me? Is this really what you want?"

"What I want is a man who can rule with me as I build my empire in this city." Veronica declared as she chugged her scotch and poured herself another glass.

"I am not going to be that man, Veronica. It saddens me to see what has become of us. You might think you are building an empire but all you are really building is a lonely self. A person who is sad from the inside and has no joy anymore. We are simply dying in the process. I couldn't see this before, but I see it now, and I hope one day you'll recognize this before it's too late." I remarked.

"You're not making much sense to me James. I'll be better off without you anyway." She said in a dismissive tone, "But I want to be with you because we can do great things together. Don't do this. You will regret this. Don't ruin what we have built."

"It was ruined even before we started building it. Now, we are just picking up the pieces of a shattered glass." I noted.

Veronica dismissed my words with her eyes and rushed out of the living room in anger and resentment. She forcefully shut the door of her room, making it very clear that she was done talking to me.

I made myself a drink, deeply breathing through the adrenaline and went to sit on the couch. I felt like people were watching us the whole time. Our voices were being stirred into cocktails of suffering, to be drunken at dinner parties, summarizing the terrors of our sorrow.

The months following the night of our fuming argument were a torturous cycle. I moved out of our apartment a few days after that night. Veronica wasn't happy about paying the mortgage herself but she wanted to keep the apartment. I told her she could have everything that we owned, including all the expensive artwork that we had collected over the years. I didn't want any belongings from the life we had built together.

Her life more or less stayed the same, except for one change – there was no me in the picture anymore. Money wasn't a matter of much concern either, as Veronica was now a CEO of an advertising agency that was growing exponentially. She was earning enough on her own to be able to cover both the mortgage of the apartment and her extravagant lifestyle.

I filed for divorce a few weeks after moving out of our apartment. There was no point waiting to see if we could work it out. Our relationship was done.

The emotional baggage that came with it felt heavy at times as Veronica solely blamed me for the divorce. She held a lot of anger and resentment towards me. Someone had to take the blame for our fallout, and I was ok with it being me. I knew what other people thought didn't matter, because what they thought wasn't going to help me alleviate my suffering.

I found a studio apartment for myself in Chinatown in the meantime. I didn't care about the size of the apartment or the neighbourhood which it was in. I just wanted something simple to live in till the time the proceedings of my separation were complete and then I wanted to take a break from New York. I wasn't thinking about where or when I'll go, but I certainly abhorred the idea of living in New York City.

Once Veronica accepted that our marriage had failed, she was willing to go forward with the divorce. She was very decisive that way. Once she made a decision, she didn't look back. This was one of the attributes that made her very successful in the business world. There were many things I admired about Veronica, and even though we were separating, I didn't feel any hatred for her. I just knew that our time together had come to an end.

Veronica was highly competitive and so was I, but I was letting go of that part of me every passing day. I didn't give her a fight. It bewildered her at first, hurt her ego but by the end of the process, she was willing to sign the divorce papers and move on with her life. She wasn't happy about the separation, but she recognized in some arcane part of her subconscious mind that this actuality was inevitable. She knew that I had to get out of her way for her to keep continuing on her path.

The months leading up to the divorce were painful. Even though Veronica and I were not in love, we shared a home and some parts of our life together. We went through many struggles together, sharing the conjecture of moments from one onset to another. The memories seemed vivid at times. The pain that came from letting go felt overwhelming.

It was an extremely uncomfortable and draining process, because of the infinite number of variables that affected the entire scheme of things. Although our marriage vows were rehearsed, it was still us who said them. We committed ourselves to each other till death do us part. It was hard to let go as I believed in the institution of marriage and had imagined a life with her.

Breaking away from those stories was a gruelling procedure. It wasn't just me, Veronica was suffering too. She was just good at hiding it as she was too concerned about her image in the outside world. At some point, when you become completely hollow from the inside, the external noise transfuses into a tide of meaningless statements, which your brain doesn't hold the capacity to process any longer. The eyes lose their spark, the body its vigour, the face its charm, the hair its lustre. Everything starts dying inside, and you can't even feel it. You do know it though, because you start buying expensive products to compensate for the failing ailments of the body. However, we stay blinded to it and focus our attention on treating the symptoms- never infiltrating through the layers to investigate the origin of it all.

My divorce was finalized in 2010, ending our marriage of almost 6 years. I couldn't keep an exact count on the number of years we had spent together. All other than the first few were irrelevant. Our divorce case was processed faster than most other divorce cases in America at the time, which could linger on for years. In some ways, we were lucky that we didn't have children, or the divorce could have been messier. I agreed to cover all the expenses of our divorce settlement, including the expensive hours of her lawyer and mine.

The days during the months of separation were simple. My small studio in Chinatown had a window overlooking the streets, a mattress on the floor, a small kitchen, and a wooden desk along with a chair placed next to the window. The walls were painted white, and I mostly spent my days doing absolutely nothing. I didn't have any possessions to my name, or responsibilities and commitments to look out for. There was no wife to worry about or clients to please. I had cut myself off from everyone. Veronica was the only one I was legally obliged to see, but there was barely any communication between us; it was all happening through our lawyers. I had given strict instructions to my lawyer that I was not to be bothered unless it was absolutely critical.

The last time I spoke to Veronica was when we signed our divorce papers. We were left alone without the company of our lawyers for a brief moment.

"Have you found a new job yet?" she asked casually to strike a conversation.
"No. I have just been on my own mostly." I told her.
"Hmmm." she said, "I am getting the place re-decorated to

make it more spacious for hosting exclusive events."
"Good for you." I said.
There was an awkward silence between us.

She was about to leave, when I said with a slight stammer, "Veronica, I am sorry for everything that happened between us. I want you to know that I do care for you and I want you to be happy in life. I truly want that for you. I don't see us talking for a while, but I hope one day we can get to a place in life where we can at least be friends."

She had a hint of tear drop down one eye. It was the first time, through the entire divorce proceeding, that I had seen her shed one. For a moment, we were able to simply look into each other's eyes and wish the other person well.

"I wish the same for you, James. I didn't want it to be this way but it is what it is. I have come to terms with it now. I hope you find whatever it is that you are looking for." Veronica stated, as she walked out the room.

I never thought that I would be living the kind of life I was living in my tiny studio in Chinatown. There was no busyness in my days, no drive in me to strive for the things that I originally wanted in life. I had just about enough money in the bank to last me a while and with the kind of life I was now living, I didn't need much money anyway. My major expenses included the rent for the apartment, scotch and cigarettes. I paid my rent every month in cash to my Chinese landlord, who lived a floor below my apartment. He barely spoke any English and never bothered me.

I only left the apartment to go for walks around Manhattan, or to sometimes go see Jessica. We always sat in the same booth in the diner across the bar where she worked. We would talk about various things; nothing in particular though, just random things. Life seemed quite odd and unusual. I was drinking a lot to numb the pain and suffering that came with my new reality.

My life had changed too quickly. My mind was in a state of shock. I knew what I had done was right and there was no guilt in me but there was a helplessness with not being able to control my emotions and life's direction. I wasn't willing to sit with that question yet. I was struck by fear of the unknown.

Drowning my sorrows in alcohol and losing myself to the streets of New York seemed like the best option. It did feel haunting sometimes, when I couldn't get a hold of what was happening. I was in the world, but at the same time, I was not. The confusion of parallel realities vied to inebriate my understanding of the moment as it was.

The shifts in my consciousness had increased in number. I would be sleeping or sitting somewhere and suddenly dissipate into a darkened space. I was learning to surrender to these shifts, which, although were bringing a lot of grief and tearing the structures of my reality, were also bringing me closer to my heart. They made me intensely exhausted though. I couldn't keep track of my days; my sense of time was fading away.

On my late-night walks through the city, I occasionally stopped into bars that were playing live music, particularly jazz. I wasn't interested in meeting anybody but liked to simply sit in a corner and drink, while letting the lucidity of music flow through my senses. It felt calming to listen to jazz. My mind felt at ease as I would sit in the dark, not bothered by the eventualities of the world outside but captivatingly sunken by the tunes of musicians from different parts of the world.

I loved how New York attracted plenty of talented musicians, who synched into the rhythms of their instruments and spontaneously played together with artists they had never even met before. I was finding myself attracted to the lives of these artists, who lived life without fear. They weren't hostage to material possessions but lived with the willingness to devote every second of their time on this planet to perfect their craft.

It was a similar kind of verve I had seen in Jessica's eyes, who couldn't care less about what would happen to her in the future. As long as she got to live her life every day with the pure intention of creating and growing as an artist and an individual, she was happy.

Engaging with music allowed me to believe that there was still hope in life, that I could potentially let go of everything and become happy. This trace of hope was the only thing keeping me alive. In the salivating space of self-loathing and destruction, Jazz became one such anomaly to my meaningless existence. Jessica was the other.

Jessica visited my new apartment one day to see how I was doing. She knew I was going through a tough phase and needed a friend. However, through those lonesome months, I had become too distant from the external world to seek help or ask anyone to join in on my misery.

I was sitting on my mattress looking out the window whilst smoking a cigarette when she asked me, "What have you been doing these days James?"

"Nothing much really... just this… to be honest." I replied casually, pointing to the small room around me as indication.
"Do you ever go out?" She inquired.
"I like going for walks and dropping into bars where I can find Jazz. Listening to Jazz helps calm my nerves." I replied.
"I love Jazz! I know some great spots, I can take you there sometime." She said.
"That would be nice." I commented.

There was silence between us. I was becoming familiar with silence. Sitting next to someone and just being silent didn't bother me. I didn't feel an obligation to speak with them anymore. Jessica was comfortable with silence as well, so it was easy being with her when I had nothing to say.

"How are your auditions going?" I asked her after some moments of silence.
"Great!" She replied with liveliness in her voice, "I have got a part in a small production. We are rehearsing at the moment.

The director is extremely talented, and I love everything about it. I love being on stage."

"I am happy for you." I said with a genuine tone. "What's the play about? And what's your character?"

"It's an adaptation of an old French play. It's a women centric piece that depicts a modern-day scenario of the biases and prejudices that women still have to face in our patriarchal society. I am personally really enjoying working on this production." She replied.

"It sounds intriguing." I said, "Would love to be there for the opening. When is it?"

"The opening is several months away. I will let you know a few weeks in advance. Do come if you can. It would mean a lot to me." Jessica declared with gentility in her tone.

"I find you so inspiring Jessica. I am not sure if I have told you this yet, but you are one of the reasons I am able to get through this time of immense pain. You bring hope and a sense of joy in my life." I declared with vulnerability in my heart. "It feels like there is nothing in my life worth living for but when I'm with you, I feel hopeful. Those are the only times I feel slightly alive."

"That's not true James. There's so much more to you than you realize. This may not sound good but going through such times of revulsion and suffering are critical for us to find our true path in life." Jessica declared with compassion in her eyes. "There were a few years in my teens when I found nothing interesting. I didn't want to see anyone or do anything. I became extremely concerned about how I looked, so I stopped eating. I almost became anorexic. My health suffered and the physical implications of this were horrible but worse than that was my mental health. I was downright miserable. This went on for a while, until one day, I looked at myself and saw only bones. I felt sick and broken but I realized in that second that nobody else was coming to save me. I had to do it myself. When I made that decision, things started getting better. Day by day, I could see myself change. That's when I took interest in theater. It helped me discover things about myself and with time, I was able to bring myself out of my suffering."

"I see now why you are naturally empathetic toward others. You can understand what they are going through. But I have to be completely honest with you and myself - it seems rather impossible to get out of this vacuum at the moment." I said.

"I think it's natural to go through this phase. Especially when you are going through such major changes in life. Embrace it. Embrace your suffering. Let it be your motivation to deepen your understanding of what life is." Jessica said as she neared my body, looked into my eyes, and then kissed my lips.

We hadn't kissed since the first night we met. Our relationship had no labels as such, but Jessica acted as a reminder that there was still hope for me. She became my anchor during those moments of uncertainty. She helped fill the void in my heart and made me recognize that there was still life left in me.

We kissed through the entirety of that night, as our bodies met to spark a chain of elation in my being, helping me to integrate the multitude of changes I was going through.

CHAPTER SEVEN

LOVE OF A WOMEN

Sometimes, one moment is all it takes to change our lives forever. Such moments are rare, but their occurrence impacts us in ways that can redefine our entire outlook in life. I never thought life would come to a point where I would become an alcoholic. I was hoping to find a ray of light that could get me out of this vicious circle of sinking into the dreads of my crucifying heart.

I knew there was a way out of this suffering. I just didn't know what it was. In the months to come, Jessica became the balm for my wounds.

We were approaching the summer of 2011. Several months had passed since my divorce. The American economy was reviving, and it would soon be a year since I had left my job as a lawyer, while living in New York as an unemployed man. Money wasn't a concern at the time, as I had enough in the bank to get by for several years.

I didn't go out to any fancy restaurants or purchase any extravagant products, choosing to distance myself from the consumerism-swathed mindset of America. My apartment design and furniture stayed more or less the same. The only addition was a vinyl player that I bought from an antique store in Chinatown. I listened to records of Frank Sinatra, Louis Armstrong, Ella Fitzgerald, B.B. King, Buddy Guy and Bob Dylan on that player, while interminably staring out the windows of my cramped apartment. Their music incited hope in my heart.

Jessica began visiting my apartment, more often than before, after my divorce. I didn't mind having her around. It felt rather natural. There was radiance and grace in her presence, which was intimating me of the good that rested within people. She was aware of the fact that I was drinking a lot, but she never asked me to stop or lessen it. However, I inherently did not feel the need to drink in her presence, and as her visits became more frequent, my dependence on alcohol lessened.

There was magic in her eyes. I had never been touched by a woman like that before. Her touch was enchanting. It always stirred something in me. Whenever I would embrace her from behind, bringing my chest closer to her back and kissing her neck gently, I felt transported to another world. She loved me without wanting anything in return. I had nothing to offer anyway.

One night, as we were lying in bed, I asked her, "Why are

you with me? I don't have a job. I am much older than you. I basically drink all day and do nothing. I just got out of an unhealthy marriage. I am not the guy you deserve. You deserve so much better. Don't you want to be with someone your age? Someone who inspires you and wants to build a life with you?"

There was silence for a few moments.

"I am with you because I care deeply about you, James." She replied with a stumble in her voice. "I can't even explain this to myself but I feel a deep connection with you. I don't care about what you can or cannot do for me. You have a good heart and although you are going through a dark time, I know you will get out of it. I believe in you. There's something about you that I find very genuine. I don't know what it is, but I can't seem to stop wanting to be with you."

"I care deeply about you too, Jessica and I find you very inspiring. You are probably the only thing that is keeping me from being consumed by my darkness but I don't want you to waste your time on me. I don't think there's any future for you with me. I don't even know what I want. I can't seem to find my footing in the world anymore. Years' worth of baggage is surfacing at the moment and it's not something you want to be a part of." I cried with my eyes reflecting my deep sorrows.

"I do want to be a part of it. I want to be there for you because I know you can get out of this. What you are going through is temporary. You can't let this phase define your entire life. You have so much potential James. I feel like I have come into your life to remind you of that; to love you for who you are and not for who I want you to be. There's a depth in you that I haven't witnessed in anyone before. I think you need to find a way to connect with this depth of yours and materialize it in some form." Jessica declared. "Have you considered writing about everything that you have been going through?"

"Writing?" I probed in confusion.
"Yes. Writing." She commented with a spark in her eyes. "I think writing will be a great way for you to let things out. Let go of everything that you are holding inside."

"What should I write about?" I asked with curiosity in my eyes.
"You can write about anything. Anything that comes out. Write for yourself. Don't worry about who is going to read it. Just let the words out and see what happens."

I gently held her waist to pull her close. She was smiling while staring deep into my soul. I had never really made love to a woman until I met Jessica. Before, it was just sex, not love. I could sense my heart expanding the moment our chests met. When she touched my face with her palms, to kiss me, I was taken aback in an abyss of timeless creation. I felt things in my heart I had never felt before, leaving me vulnerable and exposed beyond expectation. My wounds were healing every time my body wrapped around hers, allowing our skins to converge and propelling our hearts to beat as one.

Her spirit was reviving mine, making me connect with a part of myself I had been distant from all my life. I was falling in love with her. I wanted to be with her, to hold her tight and tell her that she was changing me. Her love was healing me, bringing me closer to myself and to the moment we were in. The past was being let go of and the future didn't seem to exist. A sense of stillness was encapsulating our every breath, synching our lungs to have them function together in a tireless spree of hypnosis.

My entire perspective on love, sex and intimacy with women was shifting significantly. Jessica was inciting a spark in me by loving me unconditionally with her heart. The purity in her love was melting the rusty parts of my body. It was reviving the energy centers to stimulate movement through my nerves and scraping away the blockages that previously restricted my sense of arrival in a human form.

I was feeling more human, more alive with each breath that I was taking in her presence. I couldn't believe how another person could rouse such an intense response in my body. I wanted to go explore this feeling, this experience more. Being with Jessica made me realize what true intimacy felt like.

I was experiencing being truly loved by a woman for the first time. The way her eyes looked at me, her body explored mine, her heart called me, her spirit enlivened me; it all felt too surreal to be true. My mind couldn't make sense of anything, inevitably causing my heart to surrender, teaching the self to let go of control and accept whatever was transpiring with Jessica.

Jessica moved in with me by the end of that summer. By that time, I had stopped drinking and smoking. I spent my days putting the words that were being transcribed by my consciousness on empty sheets of paper, filling the white with thoughts that spurred from the inmost parts of the self.

I would wake up in the morning, prepare a cup of coffee out of a French press, sit on the chair by my desk and stare at the empty pages on it. No words came out for days, but I continued to sit through the emptiness. I had given up on using my phone and laptop months ago, and there was no television in my apartment. Basically, there were no distractions. While the world around me was hooked onto their gadgets, I felt like a man from a different century.

Days after staring at the blank sheets for hours, a shift happened in my consciousness and the thoughts emerged. The mind began to navigate past its layers and look beyond the perplexity of living between parallel realities.

Writing helped me shift between these realities but also stand independent of them. I noticed certain peculiarities in relation to the shifts in my consciousness. There was a big gap to be explored in between the dual nature of my mind. I became aware of the subtle vibrations that my mind couldn't grasp earlier. Escaping duality of the mind for the slightest second helped me access words that I didn't even know existed in my vocabulary.

All would come to a pause as I lived in coherence with my

breath and dove into the sea of my mind to explore spaces and hidden caves that held treasures I was yet to discover.

A new dimension of the world was opening and all I had to do was simply sit and scrutinise the blank sheets of paper. Over time, the blank papers filled with words that meant nothing to the world outside, but everything to me.

Writing became a channel for me, and Jessica the enabler triggered my mind into exploring a world beyond the parameters of human conditioning. It was by being with her that I was able to release and let go of who I thought I was. Her eyes awakened my soul, which began imprinting itself on my journal.

I didn't eat or sleep much as there was this immaculate rush of energy crushing through my spine, keeping me afloat through interminable hours of writing.

"I am unable to stop writing." I said to Jessica, one night when we were holding each other's gaze after having made love for hours.

"Then don't. Keep at it." She replied as her fingers gently stroked my cheeks.

"I can't help it. Things are coming out of me and I am learning to surrender myself to it." I declared.

She gave an enduring smile, as we kept looking at each other through the silence in that moment.

"I think I am falling in love with you, James." She whispered.

"If this is what love feels like, then maybe I am in love with you as well Jessica." I said with my heart flouting its walls. "I can't explain what's happening to me since I have been with you. There's this constant expansion in my chest, which feels overwhelming at times."

"You don't have to explain it. I understand. I feel it too. We don't need to try and put words to whatever this is. Let's just be with it and see where it takes us." She commented.

"I agree. I couldn't put words to it, even if I tried. The heart in its capacity is being pushed into defying its limits. We are mirroring each other, reflecting ourselves through one another." I said.

"What we have is rare." She declared. "I have been in love before. Once. But this is different. This can't be explained to the world outside."

"There is no filter with you. What you are inside is what I see you as. There is genuineness in your eyes. It has ignited my spirit to recognize the authenticity of what two people can share. I don't love you for what you can do for me. I have fallen in love with you for who you truly are. I don't know what's going to happen between us in the future but in this moment, I know I love you with all my heart. With everything I have got. I love you with the intention of not wanting to hold anything back, of not shying away from jumping completely in this wagon, without fearing getting hurt in the process. You have prompted me to recognize what it takes to love another person whole heartedly." I declared. "There is a sense of liberation to it all."

Jessica kissed my forehead and gently made her way down to passionately induce my heart with the luring touch of her lips. It provoked ecstatic flashes of nirvana by uniting me with the energy of God in its absolute form. It wasn't God as we hear or know of but a formless sense of abstract truth where all of life seems to coexist and expand in coherence with the entire universe.

Jessica would leave the apartment in the mornings for her theater rehearsals, which were followed by her shift at the bar. From the moment she finished her work at the bar to the time she had to leave in the morning, we would spend it all together. We had enough hours during the day to do our own things, and by the end of it, all we would want was to be in each other's company.

What we shared felt so natural and real that we didn't have to force ourselves to be in each other's company. We wanted to be together. To experience the rawness of an oddity that was metamorphosing between us.

New York with its faintest shades of grey acted as a reminder of why I chose to exit my original path, even if it seemed insufferable and unbearable at times.

I would write for some time in the mornings soon after Jessica would leave. This was followed by solo walks around the city in the afternoon. My writings were about nothing specific. I simply created short stories based on intriguing people that I noticed during my walks. There appeared to be so much to people behind the façade that they put on for the world outside. Exploring the mysterious, hidden side to these imaginary characters was helping me uncover the cloaked tangents of the self. It was carrying me through an unfamiliar territory where I could let my imagination run wild and come to terms with my own unhinged darkness. With my heart falling in love for the first time and my mind breaching its limits, writing became a source of inspiration for my sense of sanity.

People became my outlet. I would find spots during my walk where I could simply watch people. I wanted to see how they thought and functioned. I didn't judge them. I simply observed their movements and expressions, their body language, facial expressions, clothes, style, and literally everything that made them distinct. I would do this for numerous hours every single day.

So much could be witnessed around the city simply by being present in the moment. Vivid emotions of rage, anger, love, frustration, inspiration, tiredness, anxiety or even hate would be perceived by my eyes while observing the varying faces in the crowd. Sometimes I wondered if it was simply my projection of varying emotions on the faces of other people or if that person was truly going through the emotion. Then again, I would think, what really is the difference between the object and observer?

I couldn't help but notice that there was a bigger sense to it all, something that connected everything and everyone, and made people function the way they did. I started observing more similarities than differences in the falsely deluded individualistic minds. I couldn't put a name to what it was that created a symphony that linked everything and everyone. I just knew in my gut that there was something more that governed the lives of every single entity on the planet. I knew I wanted to explore this sense of mysticism that was being professed by my widening eyes.

Many times while writing, my consciousness drifted through many altering courses of realities. I would be carried into distant worlds and my mind would interact with people and places that were anonymous to me before.

New spheres of existence were being shaped by the changing perceptions of my imagination, relaying me further into the depths of my mind to investigate the consequential questions that shaped the course of our reality.

Samson was a homeless black man who I met during random walks through lower Manhattan. He would always smile at me and say, "God bless you", whenever he saw me walk by his usual spot, which was at the corner of Howard and Centre Street. He wore torn shoes, ripped jeans, and a black t-shirt with the sign "peace and love" printed on it in white. He never asked anyone for money. He simply sat on the sidewalk with his ukulele, singing soulful music with a striking smile on his face, sharing his blessings with people. A hat rested a few inches ahead of where he sat and people walking by him would sometimes drop change in it, not taking a moment out of their busy lives to even glance at him. It was after my second time walking past him that I stood for a moment to hear his words and absorb the music that was strung by the rusty chords of his broken ukulele.

He acknowledged my presence with a smile and continued singing. I had never seen a smile so radiant before. His husky voice had a profundity that needed no tuning. It was linked directly to his soul and his soul was surrendered to his God.

"That was beautiful." I said to him the moment he stopped singing.
"Thank you, brother." He replied with his eyes showering love.
"How do you find inspiration to sing like this?" I asked him out of sheer curiosity.

He laughed and said, "I don't know man… It just kind of comes to me. It's what my soul asks me to do."

"Your soul?" I said in a doubtful tone.
"Yes. My soul. The thing that keeps us alive. And gives us hope." He replied.
"How can you talk about hope? Even when you don't have anything?" I asked, something in me just felt like I could be frank and honest with him.

"Who says I don't have anything? I have everything a man could ask for. And more importantly, I have God." He replied.

"God?" I said with a cynical tone.

"Yes. God. I find hope in surrendering myself to God. I know he hasn't given me much. But he has given me enough, where I can connect with him to liberate myself." He declared with pure belief in his voice.

"Liberate yourself? How?" I wondered.

"Through music, through moments of connecting with God and speaking the truth of my soul. I find it liberating." He declared.

"Hmm...." I said. "What do you mean, when you say you find it liberating?"

He laughed.

"I cannot explain it to you brother. It's a feeling, something you cannot purchase at a store. It energizes me. Sometimes I go for days without food. But when I start singing, I am able to connect to the source, and then I feel fine. I feel good, rather." He shared.

I dropped a few dollars in his hat and continued with my walking. I was asking myself, 'how could this homeless man talk about liberation with such ease and equanimity? Maybe because he has got nothing to lose' or 'Just maybe, he comprehends something that I and the myriad number of people who walk past him every day don't.'

The scenes of ubiquitous synchronicity were proof of the simple fact that my mind was expanding in its limits and dissecting past its ideas of "what was possible" and "what was not". I was starting to believe that it was possible for me to find joy in life, to discover life's purpose and live daily with hope and love. Like Samson does. Like Jessica does. These were individuals who had entered my life to remind me of what truly mattered.

It was encounters such as the one with Samson that filled my days with a brimming curiosity of wanting to discover things out of the ordinary. I was breaking out of the mold by simply enacting the words of ordinary, unusual people, who were living their lives doing what pleased their hearts. They weren't trying to seek validation from others or stood desperate in their attempt to force their will on the outside world. They were an example of living. They carried grace in their eyes and vigor in their bodies that couldn't be bought, but only earned by dedication to a sole commitment of persisting in their honest pursuit of happiness.

CHAPTER EIGHT

THE FATE OF CARDS

My encounters with distinct individuals around the streets of New York were growing in number, leading me to a destination I couldn't foresee.

It was on a casual walk through Washington Park near Greenwich village that I came across a transitory market that had been set up for a few hours by small traders. They were selling organic and locally sourced products like clothes, food, jewellery and beer, along with a variety of engaging activities to entertain the crowd. I wasn't interested in any products but wanted to observe people in this setting.

A gypsy woman dressed in an elegant dark maroon shaded gown was sitting at the tail end of the market with her tarot cards and crystals set up over a small table. Her skin was enriched with the glow of the sun and her burnished sable hair reached all the way till her lower back. She wore a silver necklace, whose core gently rested at the center of her chest. The metal rings on her finger complimented her necklace and created a captivating presence. She was a fairly old woman, but the skin on her face looked brisk and her eyes conveyed profound wisdom.

Regardless of the buzzing movement of so many people in that market, I was drawn, for some reason, by the manifestation of this woman. She carried a feel of conviction as she sat there untouched by the busyness of the crowd around her.

My feet were drawn towards her table and soon, I stood next to it studying her eyes. She looked at me with a kind of directness no one had, ever before.

"Would you like a reading?" she asked.
"I don't think so." I replied. "I am simply curious."
"For you, I can do the reading without any charge." She declared with a spark in her eyes.
"It's not that I cannot pay for it. I just don't think I will get anything out of it." I said.
"You wouldn't be here if you actually believed that. Come sit." She commented.
"Well, it can't hurt." I declared and sat next to her.

"I don't need to see your cards to tell you that you are going through some big shifts in life at the moment. Your face and eyes reflect that. But let's look at your cards anyway." She commented with bleak empathy in her voice.

There were two decks of tarot cards on the table next to the crystals.

"Shuffle both the decks with an intention or a question in mind, and then hand them back to me." She instructed as she pointed her finger at the decks. I followed her instructions but couldn't really think of an intention or a question. My mind was rather blank.

I handed her the decks, as she asked me, "Did you have an intention or a question in mind?"
"Honestly, I couldn't think of anything." I replied.

"Pick 3 cards each from both the decks." She instructed.
I followed without reluctance and handed her the cards that I picked out.

She picked the cards and displayed them in a square formation.

"Interesting." She affirmed. "I knew it was you."

I had no idea what she was talking about.

"This is going to sound strange, but I had a dream about you a few nights ago. In this dream, I was told that I was soon going to meet a man who would need my guidance, who would come to me looking for something, but he wouldn't know how to ask." She declared.

"Okay. How do you know I am the man?" I asked with curiosity and scepticism on my mind. I had also seen enough strangeness in NYC to not question it anymore.

"I can't share all the details with you. But I know it's you. And your cards confirm that." She commented.
"These are just some random cards." I said.
"There's no such thing as random. There is a reason you picked these cards out, even if you do not know it yet. It's all part of the plan." She declared.
"What plan? What are you talking about?" I was getting frustrated but equally inquisitive.

"Let's look at your cards." She said calmly. "You have got - Death, The Hermit, The Lovers, The Wheel of Fortune, The Devil and Judgement."

She began reading my cards, while I sat there quietly.

"You have ended a prolonged cycle of your life. Death represents the end of that cycle and the beginning of a new one, one that you are now entering. It's essential that you don't let fear of change hold you from this transformation. The sooner you accept the death of your past and let it go, the sooner you will be able to walk a new path." She narrated, with her palms weaving through the air in a flowing spirit.

"You have been like a hermit for many months now. Contemplating. Processing. Observing. Accepting the change and the death of your past. There's still a bit left in your phase of being a hermit, but sooner or later, you will have to get out, face the unknown and explore what life has to offer or else this hermit will play into the devil. It clearly shows that if you don't get yourself out of your comfort zone, you may fall into the trap of addiction and lose your sense of freedom."

I was hooked. I couldn't believe the words being spoken. They resonated so gravely. It was exactly what I was going through. I stayed mute as she continued with her reading.

"There is a girl in your life at the moment." She declared and waited for a confirmation.
"Yes." I replied.
"The card of lovers shows that. It clearly suggests that you are in some form of a union, which in accordance with the card of judgement is stimulating an awakening in you. It's broadening your awareness to make you recognize that there's more to life than you previously imagined. She is an important link for you in your transition from one world to another but remember - she is just a link. She won't be in your life forever. She will serve her purpose and disappear once the wheel of fortune arrives. The inevitable will occur. Your fate will call on you to act - to move on from this transitory phase and get onto an unsolicited journey in a faraway land. Your days in New York are numbered. Your destiny awaits you. You can no longer fight it from taking you on a new path. If you fight it, you will destroy yourself. But if you surrender to it and accept it, it will take you on an unbelievable voyage." She recited with her eyes wide open.

"How can you know all this from a bunch of cards? I can't just leave Jessica. She is the only thing keeping me sane through all of this." I opened up.

"Cards never lie. They show us the truth of what we already know deep down but are not willing to face. The girl you are with now, Jessica? She is a way shower. She has come into your life to guide you on to the path of light, but soon when her work is done, she will disappear. This is not my fate to decide, but life's." She continued. "Your cards evidently indicate that big shifts are transpiring for you, and they will continue to unfold even further. You only have two options: either surrender and let go of control or fight it. If you surrender to it and dance to the tunes of life, astounding things will come your way. But if you fight it and try to control your every move, which is what you did for the last so many years, you will end up destroying yourself.

Her words were carving through my chest. They were exactly what I needed to hear, but I wasn't willing to fully accept them as I didn't want to lose Jessica. The thought of losing her made me feel completely lost. I couldn't accept it.

"This reading for you was bestowed to me by someone you may meet one day, if you nurture the strength to follow through what I have shared with you. I cannot accept money for this reading, as it would be a sin on my part. Please don't insist on it either. Solely take these words with you and my purpose would be served." She declared.

I nodded my head in agreement and left the company of that mysterious gypsy woman. I didn't even get to ask her name, as I was completely enamored by her aura.

The walk back to my apartment consisted of fearful thoughts of losing Jessica. I couldn't let go of the words from that reading. They were meandering in my head, causing fear to arise in my heart. "How could this be? Maybe it was all just a story, and nothing that she said really matters."

But I knew her words were powerful, regardless of all the logical explanations I came up with to denounce them. Her reading left a lasting impression on my being. It flickered fear that enslaved my heart, for I wasn't ready to lose Jessica.

I was struck by fear and nervousness following that card reading with the gypsy woman. My mind was trapped with the thought of losing the only person I had ever loved. I couldn't write that day and waited anxiously for Jessica to arrive, so that I could hug her and never let her go.

Hours went by as I anxiously waited for Jessica to walk through the door. She usually arrived around 11 pm. The ticking of the clock haunted me, as the hour of her arrival loomed. It was 20 past 11pm and Jessica hadn't walked in yet. My anxiety had, by then, transmuted to a lucid form of panic attack. I didn't know what to do. I didn't know how to reach her. I waited till midnight and then left my apartment in the direction of the bar where she worked.

I hadn't been inside the bar since the day I went looking for her the first time. We generally met at the diner.

I arrived at the crossroads of 6th avenue and W 13th street, hoping to meet Jessica but was greeted by a sight that absolutely astonished me. There was no bar! I looked across the street at the diner, where Jessica and I used to meet. I ran inside the diner, looking for the waitress who used to take our orders. She wasn't there either. I inquired urgently from another woman, who stood behind the counter, "what happened to that bar across the street?"

"What bar? I am new here. I don't know of any bars." She replied.

"Can you ask anyone else inside the kitchen?" I requested with a frisky tone.

"We are all new here. The diner was recently bought by a businessman, who fired the old staff and brought in new people. We have not seen a bar across the street since we started working here a few months ago." She commented.

I couldn't believe it. None of it made sense.

"Where could she be?" I asked myself.

I had never met any of her friends or her theatre colleagues.

"Theatre? Yes. Theatre." I remembered. "Let's go there."

I didn't care that it was almost 1 am, but I left the diner to look for her theater. I only realized moments later that I didn't know which theatre she went to. She had never mentioned the name and I had never asked her.

My heart was beating tirelessly. I had no idea where Jessica was or how I could get in touch with her. It was preposterous. "How could I let this happen? Why did she not tell me that the bar had closed? Where did she go all this time? Why did I never ask her about it?"

My mind was overwhelmed with unanswerable questions surmounting my nerves. I stood alone in the darkened streets of New York with absolutely no idea where Jessica was, painfully wondering if I will ever see her again.

The words of that gypsy woman echoed in my ears, as I let the solemnity of that night take me hostage to its absurdity.

"She will disappear."

I couldn't sleep all night. I did not know how to find Jessica. For a moment, I regretted not having a phone or Jessica's number on me. I had cut myself out from the digital world several months ago, and now that decision was haunting me as I couldn't think of a way to find her.

'How could I be so foolish; I should've cared more. We live in NYC for God's sake; anything could have happened to her!' were the thoughts that ran on loop the entire night.

Through the course of that sleepless night, I decided to visit a computer store in Chinatown as soon as its doors would unlock in the morning to get on a computer and access the internet. My intention was to utilize Google Maps to make a list of all the theatres in Manhattan, and reach out to them to find the one that Jessica rehearsed in.

I didn't even know the name of her play. I just knew a few details about the play, such as the fact that it was female centric and adapted from an old French piece. I hoped this little information was enough to form a query for the theatres.

My eyes were waiting for light to enter the windows of my apartment. I couldn't sleep. I couldn't eat. Couldn't think of anything but Jessica. Where could she be?

The words of that gypsy woman, "she will disappear" compellingly kept popping in my head in fleeting intervals and kept torturing me.

I got out of the apartment as soon as the sun hit the streets. I made my way to the computer store which was located a few blocks away from my apartment. It wasn't open yet. So, I went to the nearest coffee shop and got myself a cup of cappuccino to awaken the cells that were quite agitated from the eventualities of last night.

I quickly made my way back to the computer store with a cup of coffee in my hands. The store was owned by a Chinese family but was mostly run by the youngest member of the family, Huan.

Huan was opening the store when I arrived.

I asked him, "Can I use a computer? It's very urgent." He replied with a firm "Yes, let me switch it on for you."

I waited anxiously as Huan quickly turned on the computer. I hadn't used a computer in months. I got on it to access Google Maps and started writing down the names, contact numbers and addresses of all the theatres in Manhattan.

Huan was setting up stuff at the front of his store, where he also sold mobile phones.

As I was searching on the computer, I asked Huan, "can I buy a burner cell phone?"
"Sure." He replied and started offering different price plans.
"Give me a cheap burner phone, with enough minutes that I can call all the theatres in New York." I declared with agility in my voice.
He knew what I wanted and brought a phone to me.
"Could you please activate the phone for me?" I asked, as I handed him a bunch of $20 bills.
"Sure." He replied.

I kept noting down the details of all the theatres. I knew that the theater she used to go to had to be a low key one, as it wasn't a big production. Once I had the particulars written down, I asked Huan if the cell phone was activated. I took the cell phone with the balance amount, thanked Huan and left the store in a mad rush.

I began calling the theatres from my list as soon as I left the store. Only some of the them picked up my calls. I couldn't find any leads and all the calls were leading to a dead end. I even inquired if they knew about a theater that was going to be running a production adapted by an old French piece but nobody knew anything about such a play, which only added to my anxiety and hopelessness.

I visited the theatres that I could not get a hold of over the phone. However, the foretelling of the cards was coming true. Jessica had disappeared and was nowhere to be found. I was rushing through a stream of rejections without any possibility of finding her.

A legion of questions inhabited the sirens of my unfulfilled demands. Hours went by as I desperately went from one theatre to another. Streets of New York never felt so distressing before. I couldn't share my anguish with anyone, even though millions abided by me, roaming interminably through their singular realities.

All the names on my list had been crossed off by sundown, with no inclination of any sorts that could lead me on the path of finding Jessica. I didn't know what to do next as I made my way back to the apartment, hoping she would show up by the end of the night.

My heart felt heavy, and my mind was disappointed from not getting the outcome it desired. Flashes of my time with Jessica kept cascading over my eyes, bringing tears from witnessing the arrival of this storm that took everything away from me. She was my everything through those gruesome months and I couldn't accept losing her like that.

"How could she disappear like that? Without any intimation?"

A bleak hope of uniting with her again persisted in my heart, even though all signs pointed in the other direction. Another sleepless night followed, with no trace of Jessica. I had no idea where she was. And as the night grew in its concentration, I only realized how little I knew about her. I didn't even know her last name. I knew she was from a small town in Virginia but had no clue which one.

I didn't even have enough about her to approach the police or a private investigator. They wouldn't take the case seriously. When I was with Jessica, I wasn't with her as a lawyer or a man with inquisitive functioning. I was simply with her as a man with no identity. Now that she had disappeared, there was no way of finding her. I hadn't even thought of the plausibility of losing her one day. She lured me so intensely that the world outside of those moments didn't exist.

"Maybe she was just a figment of my imagination?" I wondered to myself. "But then how would the gypsy woman know of her? Have I lost my mind?"

It was all too overwhelming for my mind. I couldn't think straight or make sense of anything. I knew there was something to be found through all these contingencies. I just didn't know what it was but I was willing to jump in and find out, no matter what it took. Something was demanding me to take a leap of faith and uncover the mysteries behind it all.

"Where is Jessica?" was a question I had no answer to.

The fate of the cards was coming to an advent as the mind remembered the words of that gypsy woman.

"You only have two options: either surrender and let go of control or fight it. If you surrender to it and dance to the tunes of life, astounding things will be on your way. But if you fight and try to control your every move, which is what you did for the last so many years, you will end up destroying yourself."

"I have to dance to the tunes of life. Surrender and trust. Let go of control. This is what Jessica would want from me." I told myself, as I kept staring at the white ceiling of my apartment.

I laid dormant on the mattress, while my consciousness was looping in circles. There was intense activity sprouting in my brain through the darkness of that unending night. I couldn't tell the difference between what was real and what was not. My mind was beginning to travel in and out of varying realities, keeping me adrift from the present moment.

CHAPTER NINE

THE THEATRE'S PLAY

My apartment was starting to feel like a prison without Jessica. My daily routine that was like medicine earlier had started to feel sickening. I couldn't write anymore either. My heart was grieving. Days passed in denial of the fact that she was gone. I was still hoping that she would show up at my door, and our hearts and bodies could be reunited.

After days of living in my cage, I remembered the words of that gypsy woman, "dance to the tunes of life."

Her words reignited a fuel in me and made me get out of my current state of grieving. I recognized that nobody, including Jessica, could get me out of this slump. I had to do it myself. I had to dance to the tunes of life. I had to find out the answers to the legion of questions floating in my head, from the mysterious disappearance of Jessica to the major shifts in my consciousness that had made me quit my previous life.

All of these events were causing an unremitting alteration in my consciousness, compelling me to look at the world with a broadened perspective.

I nudged myself to get out of the apartment and on the streets of New York. I did not know where to go but the apartment felt suffocating by this point. It was mid-day when I arrived outside the glass door of Huan's store. The name of the store was inscribed in Chinese symbols above the door, so I had no idea what it was called. I walked in and was greeted by Huan.

"Welcome back." He said to me with a timid smile on his face. He wore thick glasses and a baseball hat over his sleek hair that fell over his neck. The skin on his face was shiny. His eyes revealed a touch of calmness.

"Can I use the computer?" I asked him.
"Sure." he replied in a nonchalant manner.

I went and sat down in front of the computer screen. There was no one else in the store and Huan kept to himself. I inquisitively kept staring at the screen; not knowing what I was doing there. I got on Google and typed the question, "Where is Jessica? " on the screen. It felt rather silly typing that question but I was absolutely helpless. I didn't know what else to do. A bunch of results were displayed on Google, from songs with the name Jessica in the lyrics to profiles of celebrities whose first name was Jessica.

I kept on strolling through Google, searching random topics that had no connection with Jessica or the questions that were keeping me awake at night. I wasn't sure what I was looking for as I was going deep down in a rabbit hole. Hours went by when a stranger walked in the store.

The stranger was wearing a white shirt and blue jeans that fit him perfectly. A black jacket complemented his attire, along with a stylish brown coloured fedora that comfortably sat over his long blonde hair, which fell all the way till his shoulders. His eyes were green in colour, he fashioned a stubble over his white face and had a visible tan. The tan was evidence of the fact that he had recently been to a sunny place, far away from the cold and grey New York.

He approached Huan and asked him, "Do you have my things ready?"
Huan nodded in agreement.

I pretended not to notice him or listen to what he had to say but my mind was curious. There was something about this man that I couldn't ignore.

Huan went past me to enter a small wooden door that was installed at the back of the store. I hadn't really noticed the door before, or the store for that matter. Other than the displayed computers and mobile phones, the store was crammed with a bunch of hardware components that were fixed inside different kinds of computers, phones and other technological gadgets.

I tilted my neck to look at the man who was standing by the counter. He was looking straight at me. The distance between us was about 3 meters.

I was gripped by the look in his eyes, as he commented, "quite a place to be searching for something."

"I am sorry?" I replied with confusion overpowering my voice.
"You are searching for something. Aren't you?" He declared with confidence in his voice.
"I guess, I am" I replied with a slight hesitation.
"Maybe I can help?" He remarked.
"Help? How? You don't even know me. We've literally just met." I said.
"We've just met but I know more about you than you realize, James." He replied.

On hearing my name from this stranger's mouth, I felt a tremor in my hands.

"How do you know my name?" I remarked, my heart beating faster.

"Let's just say, I am a messenger who has been sent to you by someone and that someone wants you to find the answers you have been looking for." He declared.

"This is too much to process. Who is this someone? I keep having these random encounters, and honestly, I can't take it anymore. I feel rather overwhelmed by everything." I replied with annoyance in my tone.

"I understand that it has not been easy for you, James but you have to trust your instincts. There's a reason you are here. There's a reason Jessica came into your life." He remarked.

"How do you know Jessica? Did you do something to her?" I replied with agitation in my voice.

"Jessica is gone. She has served her purpose. Now, it's time for me to serve mine." He declared.

"I don't have time for this bullshit." I said in a frustrated tone as I got up to leave the store.

Huan came back out from the wooden door as soon as I got up to exit the store. I dropped a $20 bill on the counter and walked past this unknown person, who seemed to know more about my life than a random stranger would. I was beginning to wonder if it was a coincidence that he was at the store at the same time as me, when he said, "If you are looking for answers, I can help you find them." He handed me a card. "Call this number when you're ready."

I took the card in anguish and hurriedly left the store. I glimpsed at the card. It had no name on it but a number inscribed on one of its sides in black, over a white background.

My mind felt agitated and confused. No sense prevailed through these days of unknown trials. I made my way back to the apartment and locked myself in till the day's passing. I felt more lost than I had ever felt before.

Few days passed by as I stayed locked inside my apartment. The card given to me by that stranger in Huan's shop was sitting on my desk. I would take momentary glimpses at it throughout the day, wondering what to do with it. I could not get myself to throw it away, but I couldn't call it either.

After being locked in for a couple of days, my mind felt a bit settled and the curiosity within me overcame the doubts that I had. I finally called the number on the card, trying to keep my voice steady and heart calm.

Soon after, I heard the voice of a man who said to me, "I have been waiting for your call, James."

"How did you know it's me?" I inquired in confusion.
"Are you ready to find the answers you have been looking for?" The voice asked.
"Yes, I think so." I replied with reluctance in my tone.
"Write down this address." The voice directed.
I quickly snatched a pen and paper from my desk to write down the address the man on the phone recited for me.
"Come to this address today at 4pm." The voice declared and cut the call.

I looked at the address I had written down. The place was in Greenpoint, Brooklyn, just above Williamsburg. I couldn't remember the last time I had visited Brooklyn or left the island of Manhattan, for that matter.

I left my apartment with empty pockets and decided to walk to the address in Brooklyn. It was probably a good walk of 3-4 miles, but I didn't care. I had enough time till 4pm and anyway had nothing else to do. Walking would probably be a good way for me to calm my nerves.

I passed through the Lower East Side to cross the East River over Williamsburg bridge and neared the address given to me. By now, I had a good sense of direction and could easily get in and around New York. It came rather naturally to me. Months of aimless walking around the city had accustomed me to the urban footprint of it.

I arrived at the given address in Greenpoint several minutes before 4. To my surprise, it was a theatre but looked abandoned from the outside. I was perplexed to see a non-operational theatre like that one. It was rare to see such discarded sites in New York, for the city was so densely populated.

There was a breeze of discreteness in the block the theater was in and in the ones around it. The streets were quite empty and I couldn't see many people around. It was very unlike New York.

There was no name hanging outside the theatre and I couldn't notice anyone. I approached the building and saw that an old door was mounted precisely between the outside world and the inside. The door was unlocked. I slowly pushed it with my palms to walk inside the building. On entering, I arrived in a darkened lobby, with lights coming from the cracked glass windows that braced the ceiling. It was just enough lighting for me to see where to go.

I saw another door, black in colour, at the end of the lobby and walked through it. A sudden flash of light shined directly on my eyes and blinded me for a second. I instinctively brought my right palm in front of my face to shield my eyes. I noticed a figure standing directly perpendicular to my body, on a stage placed at a distance. I could only see the silhouette of the figure as the light was too strong. I noticed the seating capacity around me quickly. The space could hold about 50-80 people on the time-worn tip up chairs. I was on a walkway that separated the seating arrangement and the stage.

"Welcome James. We have been waiting for you." The statement echoed through the walls of the theatre. It was a resounding voice of a woman I had never heard before. I hastily kept walking and neared the stage, trying to get closer to the source of the voice.

My eyes were frozen on the dark-skinned woman dressed in a white attire. The drapes of it elegantly fell all the way to the floor. Her hazel eyes were divine, her greyish hair were braided exquisitely and were swiftly falling down her arms and back. Her face was beaming with light as if her body was aligned with her highest self. I was enchanted by her presence, which felt almost deity-like. I hadn't ever seen such a graceful woman before.

She delivered a smile in my direction as if replicating the moon, while her eyes twinkled like the stars.

"It's good to see you, James." She declared.

I couldn't respond as I was completely entranced by our meeting. There were other people standing behind her, people I had met before but I had barely noticed them properly. There was Samson. The Gypsy woman. Huan. And the anonymous man I had met in Huan's store.

I was bewildered to the core of my being.

"What's going on? What is happening? Who are you?" I said out loud in a compelling manner.

"Patience, James. Your answers are coming." The woman in white remarked in a reassuring yet stern tone.

"There's a reason to everything that has happened in your life in the last few years. There's a reason why Jessica came into your life. There's a reason why you were miserable in your life before, why you can't sleep at night, why you constantly wonder about the truth of reality, why you are not able to make sense of things and why it feels like you are swinging between the duality of our existence, questioning the frameworks and structures of the world we live in." She narrated as I listened sharply.

"Your instincts have been guiding you in the right direction even if they have caused a lot of pain and suffering. Every single causality that has transpired through your daily conflict with your reality has brought you here. Your yearning for answers to the questions hurdling your senses has kept you moving forward."

"It doesn't feel like I am moving forward. Or moving at all. I feel quite stuck. And although your words sound good, where exactly am I? Who are you? Why have I met all of you? Where is Jessica?" I replied with timidness capturing my voice.

"Jessica is no longer a part of this reality. Your reality. The one you are slowly breaking out of." She declared. "The world as we know it doesn't simply attune to one reality, but multiple. These realities regularly coincide with one another. Most people are not aware of the reality beyond the one they are born into as leaving your reality can be a torturous process. These realities run parallel to one another, maintaining the balance of our universe. But the reality you were born in has gone out of balance, causing our universe to lose its equilibrium and be taken hostage by the darkness that currently occupies the hearts of the people living in your reality."

"My reality? Darkness? What are you talking about? How can any of this be true?" My mind was conflicted by her words even though they resonated with my heart.

"James, ask yourself, why are you searching for Jessica? What did she do for you?"

"She.... loved me for who I was. I felt alive with her. I felt things with her I didn't even know I was capable of feeling. She opened my heart. She......" I couldn't bring myself to answer the questions asked.

"She was a way shower. She brought light to your heart, to help you fight your darkness and erase the misery in your life. Your heart was a victim of darkness and she triggered you to become aware of it. What you are really searching for is not Jessica, but that light; the feeling of hope that she incited in you, where you didn't want to just give up or give in to the darkness that had consumed you all your life. You have been persisting through days of internal conflicts because deep down you know there's a way out." She continued, "Your consciousness has always known. That's why you have those baffling moments of shift in your consciousness where you arrive in darkened spaces. Jessica simply initiated what was already in you, something you had suppressed from your childhood. Remember that time in the museum? Where after seeing the pictures of your ancestral land, you lost your consciousness or that time on Wall Street, where something similar happened."

"How could you possibly know about those incidents? They were so personal and I never discussed them with anyone." I replied with my heart tearing down.

"I know things about you that you can't conceive of at the moment. I can't explain everything to you, but I can tell you this: the moments you had in the museum or on Wall Street were no accident. You have been shying away from acknowledging a part of yourself since you lost your father. There's a lot more to that story than you are aware of. You have been suppressing a big part of yourself since his death. You have an innate ability to travel through different realities, an ability you have received from your father. Your consciousness isn't limited to this form. It can travel beyond it. Deep down you have always known this, but you have been scared to recognize it. You have been trying to play a role all your life, while defying yourself of your true potential." She narrated.

"This is crazy. Traveling through different realities sounds unreal. My life is not some fairy tale movie. How could this be?" I responded with a quiver in my voice as my body felt numb.

"Darkness has captured the world of humans in your reality. This darkness keeps on expanding and is tipping the universe off balance. You have the ability to travel through different realities so that you can bring light into your reality, the reality you were born in, the reality where people have become distant from their hearts. Evil has possessed them and they are destroying everything. Wars, famines, diseases, inequality, crimes, greed, inhumanity and destruction have consumed the lives of people living in this reality. Even your father's death was a mere consequence of the darkness taking over the hearts of people living in your reality." She recited.

"How do you know my father and how can that be? My father was just a common guy, who immigrated to America from India. All of this doesn't make sense." My brain was feeling exhausted from all this information.

"Yes. He was just a common looking guy on the outside, but that was the whole point. His real identity was never to be revealed. None of ours is. Your mother never knew about the real him. And ask yourself, what do you really remember of your father?" She said with her eyes wide open. "You didn't know anything about Jessica either, did you? She just disappeared one day. Just like your father."

She was right about that. I had barely any recollections of my father and knew nothing about Jessica.

"Samson was just a homeless person to you when you first met him but you knew after your brief interaction with him that he knows something that you don't. You were attracted to Judy in the same way. You couldn't help but be drawn to the direction of her table and have your cards shown to you." She said as she pointed her fingers towards first Samson, and then towards Judy, the gypsy woman.

I realized that this was correct. I couldn't resist myself from interacting with Samson or Judy. There was something connecting all of us, tying us together.

"People in your reality see what they want to see based on their limited perception and conditioning. When you saw Samson, you saw a homeless man before you saw anything else. Same with Judy, because that's what your mind has been trained to believe. You see things based on your mind's perception of how it labels and identifies objects – be it people or things. You are a product of this reality where the darkness keeps you distant from the truth of light – the truth that can liberate your heart." She narrated, as the walls of the auditorium kept echoing her words. Her words were shredding my mind into slices of mockery that had been my reality till this moment.

I wasn't fully able to digest all the information that was being thrown my way. It was too much for me to process. But I knew I had to find out more. There was no going back. I had come here looking for answers and I wasn't going to let my doubts and skepticism come in the way of finding them. The whole concept of reality that had been formulated in my head was ripping apart. This woman knew something that I didn't. The unexplainable shifts in my consciousness from my past were now being revealed and I was curious to find out more.

CHAPTER TEN

DARKNESS IN OUR HEARTS

Anger was rising up my chest and the words of the woman standing forth my startled eyes were carving through my skin. My nervous system felt battered by the indecipherable manifestation of the moment that I was in.

"I know all of this is a lot for you to take in, James but it's time for you face the truth." She declared. "You have been unknowingly searching for the truth for many years now and that is what brought Jessica into your life. This unyielding desire in you to find the truth of life comes from your father. He had the same desire in him before he set out on his path of discovery. He was constantly traveling through different realities to bring depth and understanding in this reality and trigger light among the hearts of the people living in it."

"If this were to be true about my father then why did Samir and I not discover this about him early on in our lives? And why was our mother oblivious to it?" I inquired.

"Your mother has a kind heart and she has devoted her entire life in service of others as a nurse and a caretaker. She raised you and Samir with kindness and love. Your father had an important role to play in instigating that kindness in your mother's heart. Not every individual in your reality can fully break free from the chains of darkness, but they can be reminded of the light they have in their hearts." She narrated. "This is why we are here. This is why your father was here. And this is why you are here."

"Who is this 'we' you speak of? Are you some sort of a cult? Also, do you mean that people won't necessarily realize the truth of multiple realities as you suggest, but they will still be able to let go of the darkness captivating their hearts?" I inquired, not able to stop the multiple questions on my mind.

"Yes James. Our purpose is to instigate light within as many people as possible in a way similar to how Jessica did for you. But before we can trigger this light in others, we have to work on ourselves to carefully understand the truth of these realities, as it can be complicated working with something we don't fully comprehend. In our attempt to restore the balance of our universe, we don't want to do anything that hinders that balance further. We have to be meticulous because we are working with powerful forces that can be beyond our control." She narrated. "We are not any different from the people outside of this theatre, except for the fact that we are growing in our awareness of the extended possibilities of what this universe has to offer. We don't operate as a 'we'.

Everyone you see here is walking their own individual paths, much like yourself. We have merely come together to let you know that you are not alone in this and that there are more people like you, who have gone through changes similar to what you are going through at the moment."

"I am not sure if this is my purpose. I was merely looking for Jessica when I came here. Having said that, I do want to understand the shifts transpiring in my consciousness since my childhood. The darkened spaces I am carried to. The obscurity of this has astounded me. I can sense that there are more people who have gone through the changes that I am currently going through; people who understand things that most individuals living in my reality are oblivious to. That's why I was attracted to Jessica in the first place, or even Samson or Judy for that matter. They had this enigmatic energy to them. I could see that there was something different about them, from the moment I first saw them." I said.

"I understand James. I am not here to tell you what you should do. I am simply here to encourage you to go uncover your truth for yourself." She declared. "You can walk out that door any second and forget about everything - forget Jessica, these people standing next to me; and go back to living your life as you were: unsure and lost about your place in the world." There was a pause as she continued, "or you can dance to the tunes of life and witness what awaits you behind the closed doors - the truth of your reality and freedom from the misery that surmounts you every day."

Fear was clamping me down as she presented me with this

choice. I knew I didn't want to go back to my old life. I was done with it. I wanted to find out more, even though my doubts were paralyzing me. They were stopping me from going all in and cutting the strings away.

If there was a moment that could redefine my life forever, this was it. For a second, I wondered if it was foolish to believe these people that I barely knew. After all, this could just be a lengthy con. But something in my heart and my gut told me to trust them. I realized I did not have much of a choice anyway - going back to my old life was not an option anymore.

"I want to find out more." I declared, exhaling heavy breaths as if I had just run a marathon, while letting go of the fears in my heart.

"Ok James. To be able to walk this path, you need to understand the true nature of the reality that you were born in. You need to understand where you come from. Before you can let go of everything, you need to dwell deeper in the darkness of your reality; only then can you bring light into it. Without fully understanding what you are standing against, you won't be able to fight it." She declared. "You have to first become one with the darkness. Embrace it in all its forms. Witness how it has overpowered the hearts of people living in your reality. How they are ruled by it. How it has corrupted their souls."

"Where do I start?" I asked.

"You need to travel east to India. Connect with the spirit of your ancestors. You have been deluded all your life by burying a part of yourself, which directly resonates with your father and where he came from." She commented. "To understand the depth of this reality, you need to first gather your own depth and how you came to be."

I felt uneasy because of her words, but I knew she was right. In that moment, I was taken back to Guggenheim Museum, where my heart tore apart from coming in brief contact with that part of the world. I had buried everything about my father and my connection with India somewhere deep in my mind from a very young age. My body was holding so much emotional baggage that there was no way I could completely let go of the darkness captivating my heart until I let go of all that baggage.

"You will be leaving for India tonight. Huan has already booked your flight to Mumbai. All the logistical requirements have been taken care of. You won't face any hurdles at immigration." She declared with an added word of caution, "But the moment you step out of that airport, you will be on your own. We won't be there for you on the path that will follow. You must face it yourself. You will have to dive into the unknown with a clear intention of sinking further into your darkness and facing it with no remorse. You can't let anything hold you back from surrendering to the entirety of darkness. Remember one thing James - you can't understand light in it's true nature till you have understood darkness in its utmost tenacity."

I was startled by the directness of this woman. She, along with the others except Huan, departed after those words. I didn't even know the name of this enigmatic woman, who had demolished everything that I thought I knew in just one meeting with her. They walked out of the backstage in unison, while Huan approached me.

"Here is your passport, ticket and some cash. A taxi is waiting outside for you. It will take you straight to the airport, where your flight to Mumbai will depart in a few hours." Huan said to me.

My palms clutched the items Huan handed me. I felt I had been in a trance this entire time. My mind couldn't make sense of anything, but I was surrendering to the eventualities of what was emerging through each ephemeral moment.

"What's her name?" I asked Huan.
"Maya." He responded, and soon vanished in the darkness of the theater.

I took a moment to observe the blackened walls of that old theater, transfixed by the lucid reality of what had just happened.

I tried to bring back my senses and made my way out of that theater. A yellow taxi was parked outside. With no belongings to my name, and just a handful of cash, a passport and a one-way flight ticket, I soon boarded the flight to Mumbai. I was flying away from the burdens of New York City.

The last dents to my life in New York City had been lifted. I got on the path of realizing the illusion of our reality. I wasn't entirely sure if whatever Maya had said to me was true but I was willing to find out. I wanted to discover for myself what really was the truth pertaining to our reality, or other realities for that matter.

Do all these multiple realities exist as part of a parallel world, which is woven into our universe? Or are they simply an array of different existences, which I could travel in and out of? Is the purpose of it to deepen my understanding of the truth pertaining to the reality I was born in?

Whatever was the truth pertaining to the equations of these realities, it was the hope of seeing Jessica once again that was gearing my drive. I wanted to tell her how much I loved her and that she was my everything, my light in this world of darkness. I was willing to bare it all, for even a slight chance of reuniting with her, of kissing her and embracing her close to my chest and of never letting her go again.

My eyes were shut but my mind was awake during the entire flight. I couldn't speak a single word since my interaction with Maya. That entire episode had paralyzed my brain and induced me in a state of mental coma by preventing my senses from operating.

By the time the flight landed in Mumbai, I knew that no one but me could obliterate the darkness within.

My entire life had led me to this moment of certainty. I had to become one with the darkness captivating my heart, and the hearts of billions of people living in my reality.

I had never been to India before and didn't know much about it either. It is the land of my ancestors, but I had no idea which state or city to go to, to connect with my past.

At the Mumbai airport, a simulated busyness of people and vehicles was visible. Huan had given me $100 to be exact, for which I got INR 6000 at the currency exchange in the airport. I had no other belongings with me. A hoard of taxi drivers kept approaching me as they saw me standing outside the arrival terminal of the airport. At that moment, my mind kept going back to Maya's words, "the moment you step out of that airport, you will be on your own."

I knew nothing about Mumbai. I didn't know where to go. I didn't speak the native language either. Although my father was Indian, I had white skin, which was inviting curiosity from the locals around me. I was a foreigner to the land, but deep down I felt an assurance that this is where I needed to be. It all played out exactly as it was meant to. I felt less fear or doubt than I had ever felt before.

I moved towards the passage where the taxis were. As I neared the taxis coloured yellow and black, a taxi driver approached me.

"Sir, where do you want to go? I will take you." The taxi

driver said with an innocent smile. He was a skinny, young man. His skin was dark and shiny. There was something naïve about his smile, and I couldn't look away from his face.

"I don't know where I want to go." I replied.
"You don't know where you want to go?" he said with his brown eyes widening in surprise.

Seeing this man, the photo I saw of the slum kids in the Guggenheim Museum popped in my head. The kids had bright and sweet smiles, just like the taxi driver in front of me. An idea came to mind.

"Can you take me to a slum?" I asked.
"A slum?" He replied with perplexity in his eyes and then continued "Yes sir. I can take you. Which slum do you want to go to?"

I was fascinated by the fact that he could speak English. I found out later that most people in India can communicate in English. If not speak, then at least understand enough for an outsider to get by.

"I don't know which slum." I replied. "Any where I can find a room to stay in for a few nights."
"Sir, instead of a slum, I can take you to a chawl." He commented.
"Chawl? What is that?" I inquired
"It is a residential building. There are many rooms on one floor. I share a room with a few taxi drivers in a chawl. Most of us drivers live in these chawls." He shared.

"Can you find a room for me in the chawl where you live?" I asked.

He thought about it for a second and said, "Yes, I can ask some people. We will find something for you."

"Let's go then." I declared.

I followed his skinny figure in the direction of his taxi. I got inside and he started driving.
"Why did you want to go to a slum?" He asked me.
"I don't know." I replied.
"You don't know? How can you not know?" he said with curiosity in his voice.
"Yeah, I don't know." I said again.
"Hmmm. Where are you from sir?" he asked.
"I don't know where I am from." I replied.

"You're like me, sir. I also come from a village nobody knows about. I left my village a few years ago and have been living in Mumbai since." He replied with a sense of enthusiasm in his voice.

"What's your name?" I asked him.
"Vinod." He said, "And yours, sir?"
"James." I replied. "Please don't call me sir. Just call me James."
"Ok." He replied with a smile.

It was night time when I reached Mumbai, but the streets were roaring with traffic. The clatter of vehicles honking past one another in an exasperating, but synchronized rhythm had my attention.

Vinod was in tune with the chaotic synchronicity of the traffic. His mind was unaffected by the madness of it. He was composed and could drive with ease while concurrently engaging in a conversation with me.

"I drive foreigners all the time from the airport but you are the first one who wanted to go to a slum. People usually avoid going to slums." He commented.
"I couldn't think of anywhere else to go. I don't know anything about Mumbai." I remarked.

Mumbai was as busy a city as I had seen before. My eyes couldn't blink without noticing a person, a vehicle or a building in sight. Every single element was interwoven to create a web of extending darkness that dangled over the spirits of our ancestors.

We kept driving past the traffic, lights and myriad of people walking by one another on the streets. Vinod was acting as my guide, informing me about the neighbourhoods that we were driving past. "This is Santa Cruz, it is quite popular with tourists." "This is Bandra, a lot of Bollywood celebrities live here." I was simply listening to him as he continued telling me about Mumbai.

I was in a very complacent mood -neither too curious nor

worried about everything that was going on. I was surrendering myself to the flow of what was transpiring.

"This is Dharavi, the biggest slum in Mumbai. Lots of tours of the slum are organized here for foreigners." He informed me, as we drove past Dharavi.
"You live here?" I inquired.
"No. Chawls are different from slums. Chawls are old buildings. They were set up during the British time to accommodate workers of textile mills. Dharavi is its own world, operating within Mumbai." He replied. "The chawl I live in is in Dadar. It is among the busyness of Mumbai."

There was something so enlivening about Vinod. I couldn't understand why he was like that. I recognized that he aroused a feeling, similar to when I first met Samson.

"How do you know all this Vinod?" I asked.

He laughed and said, "I don't know. I love learning about Mumbai. I ran away from my village in North India and came to Mumbai with nothing. Ever since I have been here, I have been trying to learn as much as possible. I have done all kinds of jobs in the few years I have been here but I love driving taxis the most. I meet new people and see new things every day."

I was fascinated by Vinod, and I didn't know why but I put my trust in him and let him take me wherever he was taking me. I didn't have much on me anyway. I wasn't scared of what would happen to me.

The wheels of our taxi continued lurching through the madness of Mumbai.
"We are now in Dadar", declared Vinod, as the streets got even busier than before with markets, people and traffic all seemingly colliding into one another. We drove past Dadar train station when Vinod said to me, "you can take the local train from this station to get around Mumbai".

We continued riding east from the Dadar station till we arrived at the entrance of many old, collapsible buildings.

"We are here." Declared Vinod, as we got out of the taxi and approached these buildings. There were people everywhere. Outside the buildings. In the verandahs. Clothes were hanging on the verandahs. Jangle of people's voices, and music pumping out of old stereos could be heard in the background. "Let's go to the room." said Vinod. I couldn't understand how so many people were living in the building.

We climbed two floors up and arrived outside the door of the room I was to stay in. People around us were curiously observing me. There were about 8 rooms on the floor of our building. Vinod opened the door to show me the room. It was a concealed box with no windows, a torn mattress on the floor, a bulb and a fan hanging on an inflatable ceiling. There was no kitchen or a bathroom. The plaster on the walls was coming out and there was a funny smell coming from the room.

"The toilets are at the end of the hallway." Vinod added. "All people on this floor share the 4 toilets that are there. If you want to avoid the line, try to use it early before everyone is awake, or late when everyone is asleep."

"Everyone? How many people live on this floor?" I asked.
"There are 8 rooms on this floor, with 3-4 people living in each room except this one. So, including you, there are about 25-30 people living on this floor." He declared.

I couldn't believe it for a second. This was such a dramatic change in my external world in just a day with no mental preparation whatsoever. It took a moment for me to come to terms with the fact that this was actually happening.

"How much is the room for?" I asked.
"I can give it to you for Rs 300 a night." Vinod said.
"Ok. I will take it." I replied.

Vinod handed over the key and a lock for the room. He asked me for an advance of 300 and an extra 300 for the taxi ride from the airport. I gave him Rs 600, leaving me with a balance of Rs 5400 for the coming days.

"If you need any help, I live in the room below this one." Vinod said to me, while pointing his finger towards the floor below mine. It was a 5 floored building, with each room stuck to the other. No concept of space was prevalent in the natural scheme of things.

The chawl wasn't located far from the Dadar train station, and there was a constant bustling of people and traffic throughout the area. The busyness of New York seemed negligible in comparison to where I was now.

It was almost midnight when I laid down on the ragged mattress of my new cage-like room. I was still wearing the same clothes I had left New York in. I had my passport and some money as my only belongings, the only two things that connected me to the reality that I was in.

It had barely been a day since I left my apartment in New York for that theatre in search of answers. And now, I was in a room in Mumbai with no idea how any of this even happened. I simply relinquished myself to the flow of whatever was transpiring through every moment of my breath. And even though I was now laying down on the floor of a prison-like room, subsisting in the middle of Mumbai's chaos, I felt certain that this is where I needed to be.

I had no idea what my next steps were going to be. But in that moment, I was glad to not have submitted to my fears and be carried along this path that I was now on. I could observe the changes emerging in my consciousness, guiding me further into the abyss of whatever it was that was demanding me to give my everything.

CHAPTER ELEVEN

A TRACE OF LIGHT

Transcending the darkness in our heart requires us to kill the external identity that we have grown up with. In killing that identity, we remove ourselves from the human limitations that restrict us to a life that doesn't resonate with our highest form of functioning.

In pursuit of answers to the many puzzles that encapsulated my recently altered life, I found myself searching for a bucket of water for a quick bath at 4am the next day, after using the smelly toilet built at the corner of my floor's building.

I took Vinod's advice and woke up early to avoid the lines for the toilet. There were 4 tiny rectangular shaped sections of toilet and 4 similarly constructed separate units of bathrooms. In the bathroom, a tap was installed on the walls to fill the buckets for bathing. Toilets basically consisted of a hole in the ground, and one had to squat to use it.

I couldn't find any bucket, so I simply sat under the tap to let the water drop down my body. It was a rather interesting experience that started my first morning in India. I knew that to walk the path that I was now on, I couldn't let any expectations or desires for comfort come in my way. I had to learn to make the best of any given situation and keep going.

The only time I got some silence in Mumbai was around 4am, even though I could still hear some noise with people getting ready for work. The people in my chawl did all kinds of working-class jobs. They always had curious eyes and warm smiles when they noticed me but the pace of Mumbai and their lives did not let them interact with me for more than a few seconds.

The chawl was like a typical communal setup. Even though I was a foreigner, people were willing to help me, taking some time out of their insanely busy lives. Within a few days of living in the chawl, I understood how integrated people's lives are in Mumbai. The concept of space and distance was alien to people living in these chawls, because things only worked when they cooperated with one another. The only time I got some time to be on my own was when I was inside my boxed room. Even then, I could hear people and conversations in the rooms next to mine.

On my first day, I left my room early in the morning to take a walk. The sun was still rising when I hit the streets of Mumbai. My mind was constantly stimulated since its arrival in Mumbai. My sense of smell was receiving impulses from all angles and the darkness in my heart was subduing my mind. I was constantly aware of this darkness, which multiplied its impact whenever it sensed a trace of fear, doubt, hate, anxiety or any sort of evil cropping up.

My fight was an internal one. Every time I felt crushed by the darkness in my heart, I reminded myself of Jessica. The purity of her heart. The light in her eyes. It helped me combat the corruptness within. I realized that I had to stop feeding the darkness in order to completely let go of it. I was aware deep down that I couldn't just depend on the thoughts of Jessica to combat the darkness in my heart. Eventually, I would have to find the light within myself to erase the roots of this darkness.

As I walked through Dadar, observing the morning hours of how the city woke up to dance to the tunes of life, I decided to dance along with it. There were small food stalls operating on both sides of the streets, where people were relishing their taste buds in the local delights. I had no idea what any of those food items were but I stood next to a tiny food stall where a bun with a patty in the middle along with a brown coloured drink in a glass was being served.

The stall had the name Vada Pav inscribed on it. I was wondering what it was and didn't know how to pronounce it correctly. A short guy came up to me and asked me in his fast tone, "vada pav? Chai?" I wasn't sure what he was offering, but I said, "Yes."

He soon brought a plate of that bun along with the brown drink in a small glass. I figured it must be Vada pav and Chai. I took a bite of the Vada pav, and a sip of the chai, and felt quite satisfied by its effects. It was delicious!

I quickly finished the two so that I could resume my walk. I went up to pay for the items and was told to pay Rs 30. I was shell shocked by how cheap the food was.

I was starting to realize that even though Huan had given me just $100, I could easily survive on that amount for a few weeks in India. The thought of running out of money wasn't bothering me as I knew I would figure something out.

It was an improbable change to witness in myself, as my former life in New York was simply consumed by the thought of money. And now, even though I didn't have any, I wasn't concerned about it. With every step forward, I found myself surrendering to Maya's words, which were freeing me and teleporting me away from the chains of our reality.

I kept trailing among the increasing crowd on the streets of Dadar till I saw the train station. I entered the train station and felt my body move, without having to move my feet. The crowd was taking me with it, and I let my body be carried along to one of the trains. I was stuffed between other bodies, as the train continued to move forward. The wind entering from the open windows was the only thing bringing some sort of respite, allowing me to breathe a little. I stayed more or less immobile till the last stop, which turned out to be a majestic station. I was enamoured by the historic walls of the station that was built in an Italian gothic style. The crowd carried me outside and I saw the words 'Chhatrapati Shivaji Station' inscribed on a pillar, on my way out.

This must be like the Grand Central Station of Mumbai, I marveled. There seemed to be many similarities between Mumbai and New York. Maybe it has something to do with the British influence, I speculated. I was soon back on the streets of Mumbai, merging with the echoes of people and traffic.

It almost felt like I had been to this place before. There was a strange kind of familiarity with everything that my eyes were seeing for the first time. Seeing all of this, some memories were starting to crop up in my mind. Old memories of my father. Memories I didn't even know existed in me.

I was starting to remember his gentle face. His kind smile. I kept remembering while walking among the busyness of Mumbai, not thinking about where I was going.

Why did I block him out of my life? I asked myself. I knew nothing about him, except his name and the fact that he immigrated to America from Gujarat, which is a state near Maharashtra, where I was now and whose capital is Mumbai.

I had come to India to connect with my ancestors but I didn't even know which city in Gujarat my father belonged to. I only knew his name, Kabir Ahmed. We never had any connection with his side of the family. I remembered my mother telling me once when I was a kid that my father left his old life and all the people in it behind as there was nothing for him there. He had embarked on a voyage, to fulfil his nomadic urges and live with freedom, with nothing and no one.

What he did is something similar to what I was doing now. The only difference between our journeys was that he came to America from India while I did the opposite. A full circle. I was starting to understand him now, more than I had ever before. I was feeling connected to my father for the first time in my life. I felt in me the wildness I had seen in him. Society's idea of settling down, getting married and living out of a framework was choking me. Without that framework now, I felt relieved. There was something freeing about it. I felt a sense of rawness, which had been suppressed in me for as long as I could remember.

His wildness and freeing spirit are what made him different, I remembered. He never could really settle in with the reality of America. I remembered how he was never home. He never hurt us, but he never explained to us where he went or why he couldn't give time to his wife and sons. He would disappear for days and where he went was always a mystery.

As the suppressed memories of my father kept surfacing my mind, it got overwhelming and I felt like I needed some guidance. I wondered if I could somehow get in touch with Maya, who could steer me on the path ahead, but then I remembered her last words to me: You are on your own.

This is what embracing the darkness is all about. I reminded myself as the distant memories of my father kept cropping up.

His face was starting to flash before my eyes. I was remembering my father for the first time since we lost him. Tears started to shed through my eyes, as I acknowledged that I never grieved him. I had never really forgiven him for not being there for me. In some way, I blamed him for our situation.

But now, I understood that he wasn't at fault. I always knew he was a good person but now I knew that he carried the burden of spreading light in our reality. He was on his own mission that prompted him to act the way that he did. His intentions were never wrong. He simply wasn't perfect. Neither of us are. By accepting my own imperfect self, I could forgive the imperfections of my father, who was just a man trying to do his best. A new light was being sprung in my heart by letting go of the resentment and anger that I had been carrying against my father.

I could see historic buildings and government edifices around me and while my eyes were engaging with the world outside, my mind was dealing with the gravities of what was unveiling somewhere in the corners of the mind.

I arrived at the landmark of the Gateway of India, bawling my eyes out. I didn't care who saw me or what they thought of me. Pigeons were flying in vast numbers around the landmark, with the sea triumphing over it. People were walking in the open space by the site but I just stood there with empathy rising in my heart for my father. I was finally grieving after decades of losing him.

It was in witnessing the darkness in my soul that I understood that my wounds could be healed and that I could ignite a source of light in my heart. This is what my father would want for me, I told myself.

I looked at the sky to thank him for all that he had done. I forgave him for all that I thought he could have done but didn't do. I kept staring at the exposed sky to let the moment take over and transport me to a distant reality. Far away from the world of Mumbai. Far away from the world of New York. Far away from everything.

There was blackness consuming my body. My eyes could no longer see the Gateway of India or the people in its proximity. My ears no longer heard the clatter of Mumbai. I couldn't fathom what was going on. One moment I stood among the busyness of Mumbai and the other, I was teleported to someplace else.

It was a darkened space. I was familiar with it by now but there was something different about it this time. The shift in my consciousness was smoother than before. I didn't have pain in my head. And more importantly, I could interact with the space. My eyes couldn't identify any object, and my ears couldn't acknowledge noise but my body was able to move through this darkened space. I felt rather curious.

I couldn't see any walls or doors. Couldn't even tell if it was an open or closed space. My eyes received just enough light to make out that I was positioned in an esoteric space, with no sense of direction for the mind to orient itself.

How did I get here? I asked myself. I had no idea.

I tried thinking about the last thought I had; it was regarding my father. One minute, I was staring at the sky above Mumbai and the other, I was here in this darkened space.

Could these shifts in my consciousness be teleporting me to a different reality? I questioned. But how could it be? How could I just magically appear here? There were still some doubts in me.

I sensed something approaching me but I couldn't make out what it was. The volume of the steps increased and suddenly, I saw Jessica. She stood several feet away from me. I couldn't get near her. My eyes were doting with joy and astonishment.

"Jessica!" I yelled.
"Hello James." She said in a calm voice. Her lips glued in a perfect smile.
"Why can't I reach you?" I cried, as I tried to reach out for her with my hands but got blocked, as if by an invisible wall.
"I am far away from you, James. I am in a different reality." She declared.
"Where am I then?" I asked in confusion.
"You are in a passageway. It is where a person can get stuck

when traveling from one reality to another. You are currently stuck between your reality and mine." She remarked.

"How do I get to you? I want to be with you. I love you." I exclaimed.

"I love you too James." She said as her image started to disappear.

"No, no. Don't go. Tell me how I can get to you." I asserted.

"You have to figure that out yourself." I felt the whisper of her voice in my ears as her image vanished in the blackness of that space.

I felt wrecked. I started thrashing and screaming, "Noo." When suddenly I was abruptly ejected to the streets of Mumbai.

Life was flowing as usual around me, and I was back at the Gateway of India. I couldn't believe what had just happened. I touched my face and stirred my eyes to examine where I was. I was at the same spot as before. Nothing had changed.

Was I daydreaming? Or was what just happened real? I asked myself in bewilderment.

It felt so real, I couldn't have been daydreaming. I was certain that it happened. I saw Jessica. She spoke to me. I felt ecstatic for seeing her again, even if it was for a fleeting moment. A ray of light emerged in my heart from discerning that it was possible to see her again. I just had to figure out how.

How do I get from this reality to the other? How did I manage to even get in and out of what Jessica referred to as the 'passageway'? I wondered.

I promptly closed my eyes, wanting to get back to the passageway. My eyes opened only to be staring at the Gateway of India. I couldn't do it.

How did I do it the first time? Accidentally, I suppose, as I keyed into the layers hovering in my subconscious mind while dealing with the memories of my father. I had to go deeper. That was the way forward.

I decided to leave for Gujarat in the coming days to connect deeper with the spirits of my ancestors. I knew something was awaiting me there.

I tailed the imperceptible footmarks of my shadow to continue walking around Mumbai and eventually make my way back to the imposing train station, from where I could get a return train to Dadar. There was a small sense of peace in my heart as I walked back to the train station, after having seen a glimpse of Jessica. Courage was budding in my chest with a deep yearning to let go of my darkness, so that I could be one with Jessica again.

I missed being with her. If it wasn't for her, I would never have found the courage to be on this path. I would have easily given into my fears and stayed in the system that I can now see was killing the people living in my reality. If not for her unconditional love, my heart would never have felt the flow of sensations it could now endure.

Seeing her face again reminded me of what truly mattered in

life. Leaving everything behind and following the light in my heart is what would make Jessica reappear in my life.

My hope of being with her rested in my continual devotion to the unknown forces that were now acting as my guide.

Change was transpiring in my entire being at every juncture since my arrival in Mumbai. Even without knowing where I was going, I was able to put my trust in the process. More so now that I had seen Jessica once again.

I was ecstatic realizing that there was so much more to life than I had previously envisioned and that I was starting to see outside the walls of the box I had been reared inside all my life. The structures of my perceived reality were bursting in flames right in front of my being.

The stars and the planets were aligning with my body to shift the multitude of horizons that previously encapsulated me. I was being called by distant voices, in a world full of chaos and uncertainties.

It was dark by the time I returned to Dadar. On my walk back to the chawl, I bought some cheap clothes and bare essentials. It was easy to find everything for a little sum of money on the streets of Mumbai. I even bought a small backpack to carry the things.

I was used to people watching me by now. It didn't bother me. I knew they were curious more than anything else. As I arrived at the chawl, I went to Vinod's room. Few men were hanging outside his room on the veranda. The door was open.

"Is Vinod here?" I asked the men.
"Yes." They replied, followed by a yell, "Vinod..."

Vinod came out the door. He straightaway acknowledged my presence with a smile and said, "Hey James! How are you?"
"I am good. How are you?" I replied.
"Very good!" He said.
"I need to go to Gujarat in the coming days." I remarked.
"Gujarat? How come?" He asked.
"Need to figure out some things." I said, vaguely.
"Hmmm… You can easily get a train for Gujarat. There are few trains that leave from Dadar station every day." Vinod remarked.
"Perfect. I am going to leave tomorrow then. Thank you for everything, Vinod." I said.
"May you find what you are looking for, James." He said with an innocent smile on his face.

I left Vinod's company and climbed up the decaying stairs of the chawl to get to my room. I put my things in order and was ready to leave Mumbai the next morning. I could barely sleep, as my eyes kept staring at the cracks in the ceiling all night. My ears had grown used to the constantly rousing background noises.

I was to continue riding on the path decreed to my spirit by virtues of surrender, with the emergence of the sun in subsequent hours.

CHAPTER TWELVE

AN OLD MAN ON THE TRAIN

I woke up before sunrise and left for Dadar train station. It seemed like I had been in Mumbai for a lifetime where time had stopped operating.

I stopped at the vada pav and chai stall on the way to the station to arouse my senses and fill my belly for the long day ahead. I felt a sense of comfort with the unknown and I was moved along the crowd, towards the ticket window at the train station.

"Where to?" The man behind the window asked me in a hurried tone.
"Gujarat." I replied.
"Where in Gujarat?" He asked.
"I am not sure." I said "All the way where the train goes."
"There is a train leaving for Ahmedabad soon." He said in an agitated tone.

"That works." I said.
"Rs 300." He said.

I quickly paid for the ticket and stepped inside the station. The train, called the Mumbai-Ahmedabad special, was to depart from platform 4 in 10 minutes. I rushed through the busy platforms to climb the stairs that led to platform 4, where a train painted in blue and red stood.

I stepped on platform number 4 and began inspecting the coach numbers written on the separate coaches of the train. I kept walking till my brain saw the number S-1. That was my coach. I entered the coach and searched for my seat number. The coach was busy. I started walking on the aisle that separated a large box of seating area on one side from a slender one on the other. There were people seated everywhere on flattened berths with no space between them. I walked to the box where I had been allotted seat number 21. As per my understanding, I was supposed to have that entire berth to myself, but many people were already sitting on it.

I looked at the people sitting on the berth for a few seconds with a blank face while they created some space for me to sit. An old man sat on one side, and a young mother carrying an infant sat on the other. There were plenty of young men, mostly laborers, seated on the berth opposite mine. Their eyes curiously looked in my direction. I accepted that this is how the ride to Ahmedabad was going to be.

Leaving the busyness of the Dadar platform behind, we were soon on our way to Gujarat. The wind was blowing through the open windows installed on both sides of the train, bringing some reprieve for the body.

The old man sitting next to me asked me in broken English, "Where from?"
"That's what I am here to find out." I replied with a smile.
His eyes were perplexed.
"What do you mean?" he inquired.
"I am going to Gujarat to find out about my family." I said.
"Your family?" He questioned.
"Yes. My ancestors are from Gujarat." I remarked.
"Your ancestors? But you don't look Indian." He said while rubbing his palms on my skin to remind me of my skin colour.
"It's complicated." I commented.
"Hmm." he mumbled. "Maybe I can help you."
"Help? How?" I asked.

"I am a trader by profession. I can speak English because I have been traveling all my life meeting different people, while trading in all kinds of products. I was once a rich man, but I got greedy and eventually lost everything. I didn't know what to do. My wife left me and took our kids with her. I was left alone and in debt. I had to sell all my belongings to pay my creditors. I had no friends to help me. I was in deep misery. So, I went looking for help." He narrated.

I was listening intently. I had realized by now that people in India were talkative and did not shy away from sharing, or asking for, personal details, even during the very first meeting. It was just curiosity that stemmed from truly wanting to know the other person.

"I had heard about a mystic living in the desert somewhere. A mystic who held powers that could help me. So, I went looking for this mystic and one day, I found him. My life changed after that encounter with him. He helped me see things clearly and broadened my perspective. It brought me on the path of light." He continued.

Path of light? That can't be a coincidence. I thought to myself. "How can I find this mystic?" I asked. Even though I was a bit wary of this, I felt that there was no harm in at least having all the information and then deciding whether or not I wanted to pursue this direction further.

"He is constantly on the move through the far-reaching desert of Gujarat. I can point you in the direction of the desert. But you will find him only if he wants to be found." He declared. "I only saw him once and that too many years ago but it changed my life. I am still a trader, but I am no longer driven by greed. I try to be of service to others however I can and live with the purpose of easing other peoples' suffering. I wouldn't have been on this path if I hadn't found him. I am ever grateful for him." He remarked with his eyes alive with emotions. "Something tells me that we were meant to meet today, and I had to point you in the direction of this mystic."

"How do I get to this desert you speak of?" I inquired.

"You will have to take several buses from Ahmedabad to get to the desert region. It is in the far north of Gujarat. The desert has many tribal villages. You will have to journey through the desert on your own. That's the only way you can find him. If you are meant to meet him, you will." He said. "I can help you get on the bus from Ahmedabad but afterwards, you will be on your own."

"I appreciate the help." I stated.

It was funny to observe how I kept encountering individuals who solemnly acted as a bridge for the destination that awaited me. All I had to do was keep on moving in the direction that was guided by the light in my heart. It furnished the strength in me. I had to keep listening to my intuition no matter how difficult the choice seemed and follow through with it. That was the only way I could keep altering the course of my life.

Once we decide to take a leap of faith, jump into the unknown and open ourselves to the world, the forces of nature rise to support us. But if we keep moaning about our misery and don't do anything about it, nothing comes to our rescue.

Never in a million years could I have imagined that life would take such a drastic turn. It all started the moment I saw the fluidity of our reality when the external world collapsed on Wall Street. Soon after, I met Jessica in that dingy bar of New York. Since then, nothing has been the same and even though I owned nothing, I felt more alive than ever.

The truth of distant realities was becoming clearer. I was starting to see how people's hearts were gripped by a storm of darkness. The suffering in their eyes was visible. The disconnection of their spirit and heart was evident. Individuals like the old man on the train hinted at what we can become if we are willing to change ourselves, our ideas and our perception of the reality that has us chained to its workings.

The train halted in Ahmedabad countless hours later. The elderly man seated next to me, whose name was Anand, asked me to join him.

"You can stay with me tonight. I can help you get on the bus for the desert tomorrow." He commented.
I agreed to his genuine offer.
As soon as the train arrived in Ahmedabad, I tailed his skinny but firm figure through the station. He carried profound wisdom in his eyes. His face was gentle and coated in wrinkles, but a fountain of youth proclaimed the shine on his forehead.

He wore a loose outfit and carried a small side bag on his shoulders that was made of cloth. As we were walking out, I asked him, "What is it that you trade in?"
"I mostly trade in esoteric crystals and rocks these days - the ones that are rare to find. They are composed of powerful combinations of naturally occurring substances, which can serve as catalysts for immense healing." He declared with a gentle smile on his face.

We were soon sitting inside a tuktuk and were on our way to Anand's home.
"Do you live alone?" I asked him.

"No. I have a wife. I remarried a few years ago." He replied.
"Would she mind you bringing a guest along?" I inquired.
"Not at all. She is very welcoming. It is my obligation to be of help to you so that you can find what you are looking for." He declared.
"Thank you for your kindness." I said.

Compared to Mumbai, Ahmedabad was less busy. The tuktuk soon stopped in front of a store, which had the name "Anand's Rocks and Crystals" etched on top of it.

"This is your store?" I inquired.
"Yes. I live above the store." He commented.

The store was established on a casual street, which had a mix of commercial and residential buildings. It wasn't too busy. I soon followed Anand towards a slender metal door that was fixed next to his store. Past the door were stairs for the floor above.

"Watch your head." Anand cautioned me as we climbed up the stairs to arrive at another door, which was wooden. He rang the bell fixed outside the door and a couple minutes later, a woman dressed in a modest sari unlocked the door.

She smiled at Anand and then looked at me and emitted a hello with brightness on her face. "Please, come in." She appealed in her mellow voice.

I followed Anand and walked inside their house. A living

room with light yellow walls and a few brown sofas accosted my eyes.
"Have a seat." Anand said.
"Would you like some chai?" His wife inquired.
"That would be nice." I commented.

I quietly sat on the sofa next to Anand. There were two doors secured in the living room on a wall perpendicular to the entrance door. They steered further into the house. His wife went inside one of the doors. I assumed it led to the kitchen.

"The bus for the desert leaves tomorrow morning. I can take you to the bus." Anand suggested.
"Thank you for all the help, Anand." I replied.
"I hope you find The Mystic." He said. "Do you know anything about your ancestors? Where in Gujarat were they from?"
"I don't know much. My father immigrated to the United States leaving behind his old life in Gujarat. He died when I was young. So, I never got to find out anything about where he came from. It is all a mystery. I have come here but have no idea where to begin from. This mystic you speak of is the only thing I have at the moment. I hope I find him and he points me in some direction." I remarked.

"You will find him. You must believe in that. It is the only thing that will help you keep going when you feel like giving up." Anand commented. "I remember that it took me days of wandering from village to village in the desert to meet him. I felt hopeless and lost but somewhere deep down, I knew I was to meet someone. I will never forget the moment I first saw him. I just knew it was him I was looking for. I lived with him for weeks, followed him wherever he went and served him. In return, he helped me connect with myself - the self that had lost itself somewhere in the swamp of darkness surmounting our ordeals."

I was taken in by the concentration in Anand's eyes. Soon, his wife entered the living room with three cups of chai and some snacks. She handed me a cup of chai and offered the snacks.
"Please eat. You must be hungry." She said.
"Thank you." I said, and inquired, "What is your name?"
"Chanda." she responded with a pleasant smile, and asked, "What's your name?"
"James." I said.

"Chanda is a teacher at a primary school." Anand said, as she went and sat next to him.
"What do you teach?" I asked Chanda.
"I teach English and Chemistry to kids." She replied.
"Wonderful!" I said.

"He will be leaving for the desert tomorrow." Anand informed Chanda.
"To find The Mystic?" Chanda inquired
"You know about The Mystic?" I interrupted.
"Yes, but I have never met him. Anand always tells me that he is the reason why Anand and I met." She remarked. "Anand always says - you can only find him if he wants to be found."

"As if he is from a different reality." Anand declared.
"A different reality huh? That's interesting." I said.

The notion of different realities was growing in its tenure, as my consciousness was vividly expanding. I was certain that I had to find this mystic. He seemed to be the reason why I was allured by Gujarat. Everything that had happened till now was pointing me to his direction. I concluded that he was somewhere in that desert, waiting for me.

After conversing with Anand and Chanda for a bit, they took me to a room where I could sleep for the night. "You must get some rest. You have a long journey ahead." Anand said.

It was a small room but very neat, with a single bed frame, few almirahs and some storage boxes kept on the side. My body became numb as soon as it lay down on the bed. My eyes were hit by blackness and my mind was carried to a world beyond the current one.

I was again standing in the passageway with Jessica's voice echoing in the distance. Soon, she emerged out of the darkness and was staring into my eyes.
"I miss touching you." I pleaded. "Can't you just come back to me?"
"I cannot leave where I am." Jessica replied. "You have to find your way to me."
"I am trying. I just don't know how to make it happen." I cried.
"You are already doing what is necessary James. Don't stop." She affirmed.
"I feel alone at times and vulnerable from bearing it all." I said.
"That's the beauty of it. You have to keep on letting go till

there's nothing left." She replied.
"Is this even real?" I asked.
"You tell me." She declared.

I was strung out of the passageway and was in Anand's house. My eyes closed to simply let the mind and body rest for the hours to come.

It was early when we left Anand's house. Chanda gave me some food for the ride ahead. I thanked her thoroughly and went to the bus station with Anand on his scooter. There were numerous buses parked in an open space, with a myriad number of people roaming around the space with their luggage. I had no idea which bus to get on.

"You have to get on a bus that goes towards Kutch. From there, you can find a local bus to get you further into the desert." Anand said.

We looked for the bus leaving for Kutch among the numerous colourful buses parked in that exposed vicinity.

"There it is." Anand declared.

It was a frayed, flamboyant looking bus with many passengers onboard.

"Hurry. It's about to leave." Anand said.
I rushed towards the bus after embracing Anand and thanking

him for his generosity.
"I wish you the best in your journey ahead. I hope you find what you came looking for." He remarked.

A man stood outside the bus as soon as I approached it.
"Where to?" He inquired.
"Kutch." I replied.
"Rs 200." He said.

I paid him the amount out of the cash remaining in my pocket, and quickly got on the packed bus. My eyes inspected for an empty seat but couldn't find one. I asked people sitting in one of the rows to make some space for me, and they did. With my backpack placed on my thighs and body crushed among that of the others, I sat on the bus and the ride began.

Moments of illusion were passing by my naked eyes. I thought of Maya and all the others who entered my life at precise moments to help me pursue such a quest.

"Was it real? Seeing Jessica again like that?" I wondered to myself.
It seemed as real as anything I had experienced before.
"I am going to keep letting go just as Jessica intimated. That's the only way." I told myself as the scenery of the land outside kept changing.

The passengers on the bus lessened in number as we began approaching Kutch. The land outside started looking more deserted with few, if any, human civilization visible. Small villages would pop up from time to time, while hours vaporized among the constant flaming of the day.

It was night by the time the bus dropped me to Kutch's main market. Kutch is a small town and at that hour, silence clung to the market. With the desert next to Kutch, the wind had cooled down after sunset and a crisp breeze brushed my face. I went looking for a room to spend the night in, as I was certain that the bus further into the desert wouldn't depart till morning.

There was a group of locals hanging out near the market where the bus dropped me. I inquired with them about a room. They pointed me towards a place that hosted tourists. Soon, I arrived at the two-story structure the guys from the market had pointed towards. It appeared rather abandoned from the outside. I walked in the door and stood aside a small reception desk. A man was sleeping on the floor behind the reception desk.

"Hello." I said in a lingering tone to wake him up.
The man woke up and said, "Oh, hello."
"Can I get a cheap room for the night?" I inquired.
"Yes, yes. The cheapest room I can give you is for Rs. 400." he replied in a sleepy tone, while leisurely getting up from the floor.
"Ok. That works." I said.

He grabbed one of the keys hanging in the lot on the wall behind him.

"Follow me." He said.

We walked through a darkened hallway to reach the nearest room. He opened the lock on the door in a half-asleep state, handed me the keys and left. I walked inside the small, boxed room. It had a single bed with cracks peeling off the walls, a bathroom with barely any water flowing out of the tap, and just enough light coming out of a tiny bulb for me to see everything.

It wasn't long before my eyes were blinking steadily at the fractures on the ceiling, while my heart was braising itself to face whatever lay on the path ahead.

The Mystic of the desert was to be found somewhere amidst the vastness of it, and I won't stop looking till I find him.

The last memory I had of my father leaped in my head as I mentally prepared myself for the days to come. He had come to visit us at our mother's place in Queens. As he was leaving the house, I remembered running up to him and tightly holding him from behind. My hands could reach only his waist.

"I love you dad. Don't go." I had said.
"I love you too, son. I will be back soon." He had replied.

I had killed this memory in my brain till this very moment, when its revival reminded me of why I was here - to connect with a part of myself I had shut off for many years. Shutting it had done nothing but corroded me from the inside. It was time to face it and witness the darkness suffocating my heart.

CHAPTER THIRTEEN

THE MYSTIC

I left my room in the morning to go to the main market of Kutch. Sun rays were gliding on the street as I walked through the vacant market. I arrived at the same spot where I was dropped off last night and noticed a medium sized old bus parked at the street corner.

The bus was empty, but some men stood across the street next to a chai stall relishing the hot chai. I approached the stall to inquire about the bus and get a cup myself.

“This bus goes to the desert?” I asked one of the men, pointing my finger to the bus.

“Yes” he said. “Where do you want to go?”
“Till the last village.” I replied.

His eyes looked confused.

"Ok. The bus will leave at 7am." He declared.

It was 6.30am then. I got a cup of chai and sat by the street to simply let my body awaken to the day's calling. More people emerged as I sat there sipping chai out of a clay cup while silently observing the still moments before my departure from Kutch.

Sometime after 7am, my ears registered the compact sound of the bus's engine. Unlike my other rides in India, this bus didn't have many passengers on board. There were only a handful of us. All passengers were from different villages the bus would be driving through. Both men and women were dressed in colourful attires and looked very tribal. Tattoos were inked on their skins. The women wore beautiful, vibrant dresses draped across their lustrous, darkened skin and metal jewelry around their necks and wrists. The men wore casual, loose outfits, with an intriguing cloth wrapped around their head and thick round pieces of metal on their wrists. Their eyes seemed ancient and their presence calm. I could sense that their minds were curious on seeing me on board.

As we left the town of Kutch behind, we started being one with the desert. The limitlessness of the desert encapsulated my eyes. The surface of the desert was thick, hardened and dry, with cracks extending throughout the land. The bus was riding on the desert itself. There were no roads, and no other vehicle could be seen. We were travelling among the bareness of the desert with the sun shining far in the horizon. I hadn't seen a landscape like this before.

In the next few hours, we crossed some villages, which were based around small oasis-like spaces. Most passengers got off in those villages. The villages consisted of tiny huts made from thick sand and wood. The wood used was from the indigenous trees that grew around the ponds that were in the middle of these villages. It was evident that the conception of these villages was a direct result of the water source that rested in the middle of them.

"We… go… to… last village now." The bus driver informed me in his fragmented English as the bus continued to ride along the desert with me and two other men on board.

The other men didn't speak any English. They only spoke their tribal language. I tried to ask them the name of their village, when the bus driver interrupted and said, "Their village… is called Maankto. They come from the Maankto tribe."

The men smiled and confirmed by uttering the word, "Maankto".

I wanted to ask these men about The Mystic but I didn't know how to. So, I waited. Soon, the bus dropped us at the last village. I got off with the other men, who were supple in their demeanour.

As soon as my feet touched the village, I felt like I was transported to another world. The village was small and did not have more than forty people. The women of the village were extremely beautiful and the men firm and strong.

My eyes were examining the scenes of the village, when the men from the bus approached me. One of them touched my shoulder with his palm to get my attention, and then waved in an inward direction asking me to follow them. I went along with them. I noticed that everyone walking around the village was staring at me.

The two men, who were brothers, took me to their hut where they lived together with their family members, who were happy to meet me. None of them spoke my language but were gracious enough to host me. I walked inside the hut, which was cooler in comparison to the heat outside. It was dark inside, with two rooms but no doors. One room was where the family cooked, and one where they slept. The elder brother had a wife and two children and the younger brother lived with them. He slept in the space next to the kitchen, which is where I was to sleep as well.

The younger brother, Amari, took me around the village after I had a meal with the family. The meal consisted of vegetable stew prepared out of the vegetables that grew in the village farm. Everyone in the tribe was given different responsibilities to ensure proper wellbeing of each member of the tribe. The tribe gathered every night in a circle next to the pond, where they prayed to the deities of rain, food, land and sun. The prayers were followed by discussions on issues and matters of daily importance. The leader of the tribe would listen to everyone and ask for a vote at the end of every discussion. He wouldn't move forward with a decision until all members of the tribe agreed to it. He, however, had the power to make the decision himself, if the matter was of grave urgency and needed immediate attention.

Till it was time for the tribe to gather post sunset, I walked around the village with Amari, who took me through their crop fields and their animal shed, where they had cows, camels, and goats. Amari introduced me to everyone we crossed paths with, and they all greeted me with a welcoming smile.

There were spaces dedicated in the village to build furniture, sew clothes, craft jewelry, prepare spices and other items that the people in the village utilized in their daily lives. Their lives were simple and in tune with elements of nature and community. The village was mostly self-sustainable, and I was delighted to witness their lives first hand.

My first night with the tribe was memorable. We sat in a circle around the fire, where they welcomed me. Afterwards, we had a celebration around the fire, where we drank locally brewed wine made of tangy fruits that were native to the land. We danced around the fire, under the kiss of the full moon and the uncountable twinkling stars that embraced the black sky.

It was a sacred night for the Maankto tribe, who believed the moon to be one of their deities. For them, moon represented the heart, and they celebrated the moon deity by expressing their emotions. They danced their hearts out in the carnival of life, while embracing the potent energy of the moon. They played their intricate native instruments and sang tunes that fit the rhythm of dancing. Both men and women of the tribe elegantly showcased their moves through the night.

It had been a while since I had let loose and got out of my head to immerse in the movements of the body. I let go and felt each feeling - the sand on my feet and the energy of the earth in my body.

The gathering continued till sunrise. My eyes basked with hope and strength in reflection to the rays of the sun mirroring over the lake. My mind was brightening and my body levitating under the clear blue skies.

I couldn't shut my eyes even after the end of the gathering. Even after everyone had returned to their huts, I stayed put near the lake to watch the sun rise, with tears of vivid emotions dripping down my eyes. All of what I was before this moment seemed to be non-existent.

Life couldn't appear any more real than what it was in that moment of complete immersion with the desert and the sun. My heart was full of love. I felt grateful for having met Jessica. My lungs felt alive. I could feel my heart pumping blood throughout my system.

The darkness was losing its weight over my shoulders and I was no longer scared of facing it. I knew I wasn't far from The Mystic. I could sense his presence near me. I decided to make my way back to Amari's hut to tell him that I was going to continue walking further into the desert. Amari was awake when I entered the hut and was delighted to see me.

"I have to go, brother." I said to him hoping he would understand.
He looked back at me with expressive eyes as if he somehow knew what I meant.

I grabbed my bag, while Amari watched me. He took a metal bangle out of his wrist and gave it to me. As I stepped out of the hut, he also handed me a bag full of water for the journey ahead. His family stood next to him to bestow me with their blessings as I moved on the path forward.

Soon, I left the Maankto tribe behind and trailed over the cracked surface of the thickened desert towards nothingness. A vacuum of oblivion embodied my spirit, but my body kept charging forward, determined to find The Mystic.

Days passed and my body was losing its vigor with every passing second. I had only a few sips of water left. My body hadn't consumed any food in days. For miles, there was nothing in sight. Not even a source of water. My feet were burnt. My skin hurt. My whole body was in immense pain. The rays of the sun felt torturous on my parched body, but something in me kept going. My functioning lungs acted as my fuel, even though my body seemed to have given up. I kept moving.

However, I was soon out of water. My physical body was in shock from the experience. I desperately wanted a sip of water. I was collapsing, and could no longer move my feet, no matter how much I tried. I was struggling to breathe.

I accepted death to be my fate. There was no sense of regret in me, for I had given my everything to find answers, with an undying hope in my heart to be united with Jessica.

With this last comprehendible feeling in my heart, my legs gave up. My knees smashed into the desert and my body crumbled. I lost my consciousness. Blackness consumed my mind. Nothing was left in me. All was gone.

This time, there was no shift in my consciousness. No arrival in a darkened space. I simply perished.

My eyes opened not to the open vastness of the desert but to a sand textured ceiling. Some kind of leaves were wrapped around my entire body. I had a mild headache and dryness in my throat. I tried to move my body to examine my surroundings, when I heard a deep voice mutter the words, "you must rest". Shocked, I immediately slanted my neck to see who it was.

A lean man dressed in a blue coloured robe approached me. He had dark polished skin, long greyish-black hair tied over his head in a spiral formation and white beard falling all the way till his chest. His eyes reminded me of exquisite gems, as if the universe resided in them. I knew I had found The Mystic; or to be more accurate, he had found me.

"Who are you?" I inquired as he came closer to me.
"You already know the answer to that." He declared with a blissful smile on his face.
"You're The Mystic." I said in a questioning tone.
He smiled again, indicating the answer to be yes.
"How did you find me?" I asked.
"I will explain later. You must rest now. Your body is tired." He said. "Here, drink some water." He passed a jar of water and helped me raise my upper body so that I could drink it.

The sensation of water dribbling down my throat felt heavenly. It was as if I was drinking water for the very first time. I decided to never take something as basic as even water for granted. I closed my eyes in satisfaction and let my body rest.

My consciousness was stirred to its maximum, bearing the mind in a vortex of spaceless creation.
My relationship with fluctuating realities was uncanny, as I had no idea where I belonged anymore.

Later, when I woke up again, my body felt at ease. It was less inflamed, and I was able to sit up on the bed. I gently removed the leaves covering the skin and got up. I couldn't see The Mystic. I looked around and realized I was in a tiny hut that had barely anything inside, except for a variety of plants and herbs. I walked out the door and found that the hut was established on top of a sand hill, overlooking the infinite desert and sky.

The sun was setting in the distance. I noticed the shadow of a camel surfacing along the gleams of sunrays, which were striking in the desert. The camel was riding in my direction and as it neared the hut, my eyes could perceive a figure sitting on top of it. I was certain that it was The Mystic. His entire face, except his eyes, was covered with a cloth that was also wrapped around his head. He got off the camel at the bottom of the hill and left the camel under a shed. He then climbed the hill. I was observing him the whole time while sitting outside the hut, waiting to finally speak with him.

He brought two containers of water along with him. The containers were tied along a rope and were hanging down his shoulders. He loosened the cloth on his face and flashed a charming smile in my direction.

"Can you help?" He asked.
"Yes, yes." I said with friskiness in my voice and collected one of the containers of water from him.

I followed him inside the hut, where we placed the containers next to the tiny kitchen, in company of all the other plants and herbs.

"How did you find me?" I asked him as we placed down the containers.
He acknowledged my question with a smile and asked.
"Would you like some tea?"
"Tea sounds nice." I replied.
"Great. Wait for me outside. You don't want to miss the sunset." He declared while giving me another smile.

I silently conformed and walked out of the hut. The sun was about to drop down the horizon, the sky was covered in red, and the desert was reflecting the solace of my spirit. It was surreal.

The Mystic came out of the hut with two cups of tea in his hand. He handed me a cup and sat next to me. We were sitting on the floor, with our backs resting on the wall of the hut, and eyes overlooking the redness embodying the sky.

There was silence between us for eternal moments.

"I knew you were searching for me." He said with his deep voice. My body was almost shaking and my mind was dazed. "Your body had collapsed in the desert when I found you. I brought you here on my camel and treated you. Your body needed to heal; it was in a state of shock and trauma. You were unconscious for several days, but I knew you would make it. Your spirit was alive, even when your body was giving up."

I was silent.

"You have come from far away to connect with your ancestral land. Isn't that right?" He asked.

"Yes." I responded. "But I no longer know where I am from, or where I belong. I cannot keep a grip on what is real. My consciousness is shifting extensively. I am not able to understand it."

"It's ok to not be able to understand anything. Before things start to make sense, they must fall apart. That is what has been happening with you. What's real and what is not isn't the question. Who we are regardless of whatever shift transpires in our consciousness is what we need to know. Only then can we free ourselves from being a prisoner to whatever illusory reality we find ourselves in." He said.

"My mind uncontrollably keeps travelling to distant spaces, where the reality I was born in seems inconsequential. Going into these spaces has made me question everything. It is why I came looking for you. I want to understand what's happening to me." I replied.

"To understand what's happening, you need to go deeper in yourself. You gave your everything in trying to find me. I now know that you are eagerly determined. You will need this resolve of yours to get through what lays ahead." He continued. "Tonight, we will be drinking an extract out of a sacred plant that is native to this desert. It is a very rare plant to find. The plant is very potent and is one of the oldest living beings with powers that can transcend us from this reality to others."

I was listening attentively.

"The plant will test your capacity. This is where you will need that fortitude of yours. Many who drink the brew of the plant never come back. Their bodies can't handle its power. The plant leaves no stones unturned in uplifting your spirit out of the body, and forces you to face all your demons. That's why it's essential that you drink it with a powerful intention to get answers to what you are seeking. The intention you set aside before drinking the sacred plant will be of immense help to you when you are dealing with your shadows. It is difficult to say what will happen to you, as the plant works differently on everyone but it will certainly take you to a faraway place and show you what you need to see."

I silently nodded my head in agreement.

The Mystic left me in the company of the desert to go prepare the brew of the sacred plant for our night's invasion of a reality beyond this one. I didn't know what to expect or hope for. I simply sat through those hours staring at the sky, observing the change in its shade from light to dark and the emergence of a million stars.

My intention was to connect with my father and my ancestors. In order to understand myself better, I had to understand where I come from. Till now, a big part of me was unknown to me. I was only aware of just one side of the story. To feel complete in myself, it was essential that I found out more about my origin. I wanted their help to unpuzzle the equations of what led to the dramatic changes in my consciousness, propelling me to leave my old life behind and bring me on this unyielding quest of figuring out the varying tangents of my altering self.

"It is time." The Mystic declared as I sat outside the hut gazing at the stars.

"If you walk down the hill towards the shed, you will see a

pile of wood stacked there next to the camel. Bring the wood. We will create a fire here." He instructed.

I followed his directions and trekked down the hill to bring the stack of wood. I arranged the wood outside the hut where we were to sit for the night. The Mystic handed me a flamed piece of wood from the kitchen, and I used it to ignite the fire.

He brought the brew of the sacred plant in a clay jar and placed it next to the fire. Both of us sat next to the fire in a lotus posture facing one another.

"The fire is sacred. So is the sky. The desert. The moon. The stars. And the plant we are about to drink. We need to show our respect by praying to these creations first." He declared.

We shut our eyes for a moment to pay our respect.

"I will be of help to you during the night when you need me. But remember, this is your journey. You will have to go through it on your own. Whatever comes, comes. Face it with the strength and wisdom of a warrior." He commented, his eyes piercing through my heart.

The Mystic stood up with the jar in his palm and asked me to open my mouth. He then poured the brew into my mouth. It tasted unlike anything I ever had before. The brew was dense and warm. It gradually melted down my throat and I could feel it spreading in my veins as my body started to feel numb. I collapsed on the ground. The Mystic covered my body with sand, except my face so that I could breathe. The spirit detached from my body and carried me away from this reality.

I just about entered a space beyond the unknown when I saw my father emerge. It wasn't like the spaces I had been in before. This one was more elaborate. I wasn't in some sort of a passageway, but an altered reality, where the desert was still in front of me, but the colours had changed. The sand wasn't golden, but black. The sky was maroon. The moon black. The stars golden. I couldn't inhale air. There was no wind. There was a prevailing sense of emptiness.

My father was standing in the middle of the desert. I couldn't believe it. I didn't even remember his face. I walked to get closer to him.
He smiled at me and said, "How are you son?"
"Is this really you, father?" I inquired, as I walked towards him.
"Yes. It's me. Finally, we meet again." He said.
"I thought I had lost you forever." I yelled.

"We never really die, son. Our spirits live on forever." He declared.

"Where are we now?" I asked.
"We are in a different reality. My spirit arrived here when it left my body." He declared.
"Have you been here the whole time since you left us?" I asked.
"Yes. This is where people who supposedly die in your reality come." He responded with a gentle smile.
"How many such realities are there?" I inquired.

"Countless. We are always going in and out of different realities. When people in your reality go to sleep, the dreams they have are of them traveling to altered realities. They are as real as anything can be." He said.

"But can they travel to these realities when they are awake?" I asked.

"What does it even mean to be awake? Most people in your reality are sleeping with their eyes open. To be able to realize the truth of multiple realities, we have to let go of everything that we think we know and that's a hard ask from people living in your reality." He said.

"I have been on this roller-coaster of a ride, where I am realizing that I do not know myself at all. I have had these moments where I am teleported to a darkened space. Ever since that started happening, I could not be bound to my reality. I knew there was something more to the story." I continued. "For the longest time, I blamed you for everything and killed this part of me. I did not realize that whatever you did was for our good. It was only when it ended up almost killing me that I realized that I need to connect with you and our ancestors to understand myself."

"As far as I can tell, you're far from being killed. There's so much light in you, James. So much good. I still remember the day you were born. It was the most joyful day of my life." He declared. "You're only beginning to realize your true potential, now that you're seeing the truth of your reality. You can witness how people living in it have lost their connection to the light within them. You can see how unhappy, greedy and selfish they have become. Love and humanity are as if lost from their life."

I had tears in my eyes.

"That also includes me, father. What happened to me? Why did I lose this light you speak of?" I asked

"You never lost it. You cannot. I couldn't tell you when you were still a child, but we come from a legacy of light showerers. It is our duty to bring light in the world when darkness surmounts it. That's why your consciousness keeps on shifting to carry you to distant spaces, to trigger the realization of the illusion that surmounts your reality. You suppressed your true calling for the longest time, but now you are here to embrace your truth." He said. "I apologize that I couldn't be there for you, to guide you further on this path. But it makes me happy to see you here and connect with the truth of who you are. We come from a tribe in the desert. The people of our tribe have been blessed by the spirit of the desert. Your grandfather was born in this desert. He migrated from here to share his light with the world outside the desert. I went to America to do the same. We are the children of light. For thousands of years, the people of our tribe have been traveling to distinct parts of your reality to spread that light. Now, you have come back here to be reminded of your purpose. To grow in the light that is already within you."

I listened intently as he continued.

"All you needed was to be triggered of your mission and

now that you are on this path, the light will take care of you. It will help you every step of the way. You simply have to always believe in it and the darkness of your reality will seem negligible. You will be able to prevail over every obstacle and challenge that may surface." He declared.

"Will I also be able to travel to other realities?" I inquired.

"Over time that will be possible but at the moment, your focus needs to be on your reality. The darkness in your reality is overpowering the light and the universe is off balance. Your purpose to be a light showerer for the people in your reality is of more importance than ever before." He narrated.

"How do I be a light showerer for the people in my reality?" I inquired.

"By doing exactly what you are doing now. The first step is for you to recognize the light within. Once you learn to harness your light, you need to nurture it to spread it among others. Your light, when fully evolved, will act as a beacon of hope for others. Your mere existence will remind them of what it means to be truly alive." He recited.

There was an abrupt jolt.

I was shaken as my spirit re-entered my physical body. I was overcome by darkness. I wasn't in that altered reality anymore. My body couldn't hold the force of the plant. I had lost the connection with my father. An endless stream of blackness surrounded my body. I couldn't control anything.

"Breathe… Breathe…. Breathe…." I heard these words echo in my ears. It was The Mystic. He held my palms and shoulders. "Keep on breathing. Don't stop." He instructed.

I had been triumphed by the darkness in my heart. All the world seemed to have collapsed. My heart stopped beating. I could no longer breathe. I felt empty. My body gave up. I crumbled.

CHAPTER FOURTEEN

THE CALL OF MY ANCESTORS

The deepest parts of my body came to life as my consciousness rose from the dead. Tears were dripping down my eyes, as I screamed to everyone but no one in particular, "take everything from me, I have nothing to give you anymore."

Nothing physical seemed to matter anymore. Whatever was left of me was being burnt away in flames with every tear falling from my eyes.

"Breathe.. Breathe…Keep on breathing…." reiterated the Mystic.

I couldn't feel my body. It simply acted as a tide of energy with nothing holding it down. Light sparked in my heart and allowed me to witness the shadows encircling my being.

“You can go back to the altered reality if you wish”, declared the Mystic.

I shut my eyes and let the spirit be guided away from the physical world to re-enter the space beyond the unknown.

It arrived in the same desert as before. I couldn’t see my father though.

“Father? Are you still here?” I screamed.
“Yes. I am here. I never left.” I heard these words reverberate as his image resurfaced.
“I was afraid that I lost you again.” I cried.

“You can never lose me, James. Our bond is sacred. You can always find me in your heart.” He declared with a generous smile.

“I think my time here is about to end.” I said with grief surfacing my eyes.

“Yes. You have to return to your reality. There’s plenty for you to do there. Take everything I have told you with you. It will provide you with strength on your path ahead.” He remarked.

“How can I see you again father? I will need your guidance on my path.” I cried.

“Everything that is there for you to find is already held inside you. You are stronger than you realize, wiser than you think.” He declared.

"Where do I go next from here?" I asked.

"You now know where you come from, and the lineage that you carry in yourself. It's time for you to discover your own truth beyond everything and everyone, and to live your purpose as a light showerer." He stated. "You will find the path ahead, the same way you found me. Just remember to stay true to who you truly are, regardless of how much the world around you tries to change that."

His voice went away with the darkness as I returned to my body.

"Breathe… Breathe…focus on your breath," said the Mystic.

I followed the Mystic's instructions as my spirit enlivened my body. I lifted my upper body to hold the Mystic, who had been chanting powerful mantras the whole time. Tears were still dripping down my eyes, as I held the Mystic's hands to be present in the reality that I was in. My eyes perceived my surroundings - the desert, the moon and the sky, as they were before. I could feel the wind striking my face. I could breathe again.

I had been reunited with my father to be reminded of my purpose. I felt grateful towards my ancestors for bestowing me with such a legacy. For the first time in my life, I could truly see my purpose clearly.

The shadows hovering around the body seized me. The evils webbed my system. I was submerged in the darkness consuming all the people living in my reality. I had never seen it from so close before. It was vile. It had no name or shape attached to it. It was pure evil in its formation. But even though I had become one with the darkness, it no longer scared me. I was learning to observe the darkness from external perspective even when it had entirely clutched my body. Death no longer threatened me. Each and every cell of my being was awakened.

I got on my feet and stared at the fire burning next to us and the stars shining in the sky above us. The moon was glowing at its full capacity. I was one with all life around me. I felt liberated to the core of my being. I understood that to harness my light in its utmost tenacity, I had to witness this darkness.

I let my feet be guided to become one with the desert. My body planted itself like a tree and my heart began to swirl like the sea. There was no separation between the land and me. All of life was transmuting from the inside and radiating along with the spirit that possessed the land. I began dancing to the hymns being sung by the Mystic, who was infinitely connected to the universe.

I felt freer than I had ever felt before. Nothing was attaching me to the body.

I wasn't chained by the illusion of multiple realities. I stood beyond them. I stood beyond what was real. I stood beyond everything, growing in the oneness of it all. My eyes glazed to the burning fire as I felt strengthened in myself. The ego had melted so there was no sense of "I" left.

I thanked Jessica for bringing me on this path but in that moment of pure emancipation, I let her go. I still loved her, but without wanting her. I realized that the absolute power of love enacted beyond any self-constructed ideas or conditions and that I didn't have to physically unite with her, for our spirits were eternally intertwined, no matter which reality we persisted in. I let go of my desire to physically be with her, as I realized that she, like my father, would always be in my heart. Jessica evoked the source of light that rested within me.

My desire of wanting to be with her rose from an unfulfilled place in myself. And now, as I could comprehend that nothing external, including Jessica, could fill the void in my guts, I reckoned that to completely dissolve myself of all human parameters, I had to continue moving forward on my own.

It was a solo journey into the unknown, where individuals such as Jessica, Maya, the Mystic, and my father had acted as temporary guides till this moment; but now, I had to walk on my own. No one outside of ourselves can provide us complete liberation from the darkness within.

Tears kept dripping down my face, as I dropped down to my knees to thank the Mystic for all he had done. The Mystic put his palms over my head to grant me his blessings, while I thanked him for helping me get through the intensity of those infinite moments. My heart was full of immense gratitude for every single person who had incited in me the audacity to leave my old miserable life behind and bring me on this path of wholesome expansion.

The sun was about to rise. The night was fading in its glory to give birth to a new day. A new life. A new way.

I sat down allowing the rising sun to let its rays infiltrate my newly enhanced system and bring respite to my body from all it had been through over the course of the night.

"I need to keep on moving." I told the Mystic, as our eyes kept gazing at the sun rising over the vast desert.

"I know." He responded with a gentle smile. "If you walk that way, you will arrive at a village of *banjaras*[1] in about 1-2 days. The village is at the border of Gujarat and Rajasthan. From there, you can find a ride that will take you further into Rajasthan."

"I can't thank you enough for all that you have done for me." I said with appreciation pouring out of my heart.

He smiled and said, "I am simply performing my duty. And now, you need to live with the seeds of freedom that you have received. The sacred plant of the desert has healed you of your evils. It has nurtured you with the strength and wisdom of a warrior. Take this clarity with you on your path ahead. Let the truth inside be your anchor through all obstructions."

---

[1] Nomadic tribes

After having lived thousands of lives in one night, I left the Mystic's hut in the direction of the village of banjaras.

My mind was in a trance through the entire walk. I was still feeling the effects of the sacred plant in my system. My body had changed in its biology. My consciousness was consistently expanding. I was mindful of the changes that were transpiring through me.

It was after two days of walking through the stillness of the desert, as the Mystic had suggested, that I arrived in a tiny village. I didn't know what day or date it was, wasn't even sure of the year. Like the old explorers, the only way I knew it had been two days by the time I arrived at the village was by observing the exchange of roles between the sun and moon.

The sun was setting in the distance by the time I reached the village. However, calling it a village wouldn't be an appropriate bid because it was more an amalgamation of several tents. My gaze met some other very curious ones. The people wore flamboyant attires and had dark skin. They had plenty of camels with them and from the looks of it, they were preparing to move soon. They were packing their belongings in large metal containers. A man was instructing them.

I approached him, and asked, "Hello, where are you going?" He looked surprised to see me emerge from nowhere.

"We are moving that way. A storm is expected in the coming days." He responded while pointing his finger in a certain

direction, and hesitatingly speaking in broken English. It was, however, enough for me to understand.
"Are you going towards Rajasthan?" I inquired.
"Yes, yes. Rajasthan." He replied in an excited tone.
"Would it be possible for me to join?" I asked, while using my palms to make him understand. "I can help in return."

He thought about it for a second.

"Yes, no problem. We can take you." He replied while nodding his head.
"Thank you." I said with a tender smile.

I helped them load their stuff on the camels, including their tents, which had to be pulled out from the grounds. In a few hours, in the darkness of the night, we were on our way to Rajasthan. We couldn't delay leaving and had to leave at night, as once the storm hit the desert, it would have been extremely challenging to even walk. The leader of the group, Aman, told me that we got lucky with the storm and left at the right time.

We arrived in an old town in Rajasthan after a few days of riding the camel. Aman helped me find a place where I could spend the night. It was the house of a local man, who was also quite bewildered to see me at first. By now, I was accustomed to the look of astonishment in people's eyes.

"A bus will leave tomorrow morning for Jodhpur. From there, you can find a train for anywhere in India." Aman told me, before leaving.

Being in this town brought me back in touch with some form of modern-day human civilization. I got on the timeworn bus the next morning, after a good night's sleep, and soon, was on my way to Jodhpur to flow with the next part of this mind-altering odyssey.

With the bus moving further into Rajasthan, the busyness of India began dominating my senses.

Something had changed in me though. Something I couldn't put words to. I simply knew I had to further investigate this change and sit with it to understand it better. Uniting with my father had healed my inner most wounds and facilitated a profound understanding of where I come from. Jessica didn't appear in my thoughts anymore. I didn't feel attached to any person or thing.

Now, it was time to experience life without being chained by darkness. My guide was the light emerging out of the core of my being. My aim was to further contribute this light to spur others by not reeling into fear.

I wasn't sure where to head next. The feeling of wanting to be still and explore the inner self was growing in me. The desert had instigated the awakening of my spirit and ignited the light within. I wanted to understand these changes further.

The bus dropped me near the train station of Jodhpur, which

is a busy city. Even though I did not know anything about it, I could tell Jodhpur is a historic city, as my eyes saw many old landmarks, such as a mammoth fort, established on an elevated hilltop overlooking the city.

I couldn't stay any longer in the desert, I had to keep moving. So, instead of looking for a room for the night in Jodhpur, I went straight to the train station to move to another place.

It was dark when I entered the station. I went to inquire at the ticket counter. A man was dozing behind it. There were others sleeping on the floor of the station. I said in a high-pitched voice, "Hello… hello..." to wake up the guy sleeping behind the counter.

He woke up to look at me with tired eyes.
"Yes?" he said.
"When is the next train leaving?" I inquired.
He looked at the train charts next to him, and replied, "Chamba Express will be arriving soon."
"Hmm. The train will go till Chamba? Where is Chamba?" I asked.
"Yes. Chamba. It's far away. All the way up in the mountains." He stated.
"Mountains? Huh? Give me a ticket." I said.
"Rs.500." He declared.

I handed him the cash out of the little money that I had left on me. I grabbed the ticket and went inside the platform to wait. There were four platforms in this station, and my train was to arrive on platform one. The platforms were less busy compared to the other train stations in India. People were sleeping on the few benches put on the platform.

I didn't have to wait long for the train to arrive. It halted for only a few minutes, and I quickly got inside. The train wasn't that occupied either and unlike the last time, I didn't have to share my seat with other people. I flattened the body to rest on my designated berth.

I let my eyes doze off till the morning. My ears were aware of the background noise being generated by the continuous friction between the train wheels and the metal tracks. My mind was experiencing a different kind of living where even when my eyes were shut, I was awakened inside, aware of the constant changes transpiring through my being.

I had never been to the mountains before. I had only seen them in pictures. I looked out the windows when my eyes opened in the morning, to find the image of the mountains embodied in a fluctuating scenery. We had crossed the flatlands while I was resting. Few men were sitting on the berth opposite mine.

"How far are we from Chamba?" I asked them.
"Not far." One of them said. "We should reach Chamba soon."
"Great." I said with delight.

I kept staring out the windows, eyeing the mountains. I felt extremely connected to their energy. They delivered a sense of stillness and stability. I was incessantly experiencing intense shifts in my being and felt an indescribable urge to start climbing those powerful mountains.

Soon, the train halted in Chamba. I got out of the train, stretched my body amidst the compact but crowded train station, which the mountains were encircling. I walked out of the station and went to the clustered market built alongside a slender street. Chamba is a small town. The locals were dressed in their ethnic woollen attires, to protect themselves from the cold. Their skin was much lighter compared to that of the people in the desert.

The crisp breeze of mountains incited chilliness in my body. I bought a thick woollen jacket and a hat from one of the vendors on the street and then engaged my senses in a meal and chai to please my stomach. I was about to run out of cash, but I didn't feel worried.

Since Chamba is built on a mountain, the street was settled at an angle. I couldn't hold the urge to climb the mountains so I started walking up to the market. I saw a bus stand several minutes into my walk. The driver of the bus was honking to get the last set of passengers on board.

I quickly rushed my feet to talk to the conductor standing outside the bus.
"This bus is going up the mountains?"
"Yes." He replied.

I didn't care where the bus was going, as long as it was riding up the mountains. I hastily got on. Soon, we left Chamba behind and rode upwards. The path of the moving bus was created all around the mountains that stood strong and stable in their grand capacity. My lungs soon felt the difference due to the elevation but my eyes were completely bewitched by the Himalayas.

It was dusk by the time the bus arrived at the last stop which was a town much smaller than Chamba. The bus dropped me a little far from the main town area, so I quickly trekked up the mountain, not wanting to miss the sunset.

I gaspingly arrived at the top of the mountain and saw a beautiful green valley resting ahead. My eyes were enamoured by the dense jungle flourishing in the valley. Vivid trees spread throughout the valley created a magical delight for the eyes. Beyond the valley was a mammoth snow-capped peak. It was, as if, reaching for the sky. As it descended, the sun struck its colours on the peak. Without a flicker of doubt, I knew I had to climb it.

I waited on top of that mountain till sunset and then ran back to the town to find a place to crash for the night. I inquired from some locals on the street, who directed me towards the house of a person who hosted travellers.

I found the house and the owner provided me with a room and food for the night. I gave him the last sum of cash I had left on me and went to my room to get some rest. My body was levitating with the energy of the mountains. Everything felt amplified. My heart felt expanded through it all, with an abundance of joy flowing in my veins. I couldn't really sleep that night. My mind was awakened beyond understanding.

I was on the trail to the epic valley as soon as the sun rose. I wanted to distance myself from human civilization and be in complete equanimity.

The jungle was rich in its natural habitat. The trees were magnificent with a variety of them swaying in all directions, fostering a tranquil energy field. On my trail, I heard birds singing and occasionally saw monkeys, deers and wild pigs. I wasn't sure which animals considered that jungle as their home. But somehow, I didn't sense fear surge in me, as I knew that this is where I was meant to be.

I walked all day through the jungle till I found a village on my way. On seeing me walk in, dogs started barking. There were only a few huts crafted out of mud and stones, in the village.

I stayed in the village for the night with a family who was happy to host me.

The man of the family asked me, "Where are you going?" while we were eating dinner in the compact space inside their hut.
"To that peak." I had said.
"Oh." he replied, while his eyes widened. "Nobody comes back from there." As he said that, silence engulfed the walls of his hut.

There was no going back now. There was nowhere to go

back to now. There was only one way to go, no matter what it brought. I had been chained by fear my whole life, and now that I could breathe beyond it, nothing seemed to matter other than the truth of wanting to deepen my experience of living life wholeheartedly through every single moment of its creation.

CHAPTER FIFTEEN

THE ZEN MASTER

I left the village in the morning just as the sun was rising. I thanked the man and his family for their warmth. “May God be with you” the man said to me, waving goodbye.

I kept following the trail through the jungle in the direction of the peak. My chest was full of emotions every time I got a peek at it through the gaps between the trees.

I walked all day till I heard the sound of children at a distance. I thought it was coming from another village. So, I trailed the direction of the voices, hoping to find a place to stay for the night. As I neared the voices, strikingly crafted tree houses came to my view, followed by an open space with a farm, green houses, cattle, goats and even horses roaming around. Architecturally resounding edifices fashioned out of wood were spread around the open space. I saw some kids, dressed in white robes, running around. As soon as I stopped near them, they regarded me with inquisitive eyes.

I wasn't sure what this place was, so I kept walking till I saw a dome-like structure in the middle of the space. It looked enthralling. I went to the dome and discreetly peeked inside the large wooden doors.

Individuals, both men and women of all ages, were dressed in white robes and sat in the lotus posture facing a man who sat at the front. Their eyes were sealed and they were in a state of deep meditation. It was absolutely silent. A sense of concentrated energy was being generated inside the dome. I wasn't sure what the place was, but I wanted to find out more. Was it a monastery? A temple, maybe? I didn't know.

I sat outside the dome waiting for the silence to end. The entrance of the dome was directly perpendicular to the mountain peak that I wanted to climb. My eyes were mesmerized by the stillness of the peak, and my body could feel the heightened vibration resonating in this enchanted space.

The sun was setting behind the mountains and the sky was gleaming in amending shades of red. Soon, I heard the sound of a gong inside the dome.

The doors opened soon after. People dressed in white robes started walking out of the dome with peaceful and calm faces. I got up to stand aside, and silently observed them. Most of them took notice of me but did not react to me being there. They continued walking down the dome, towards a congregation hall placed further away from the fields.

I waited for the man, who they were all facing while meditating, to walk out. He didn't exit the dome even after everyone left. So, I approached the door again to check inside. He was still sitting in a lotus posture with his eyes closed. I took off my shoes and left my backpack outside and silently walked inside to sit down on the floor, in front of this man.

I hadn't seen a face so calm before. He had a bald head and luminous skin. His body was covered in a white robe, just like the others. His face was full of life and there was an unparalleled aura to his presence.

I kept sitting inside the dome, which was painted all white from the inside, till this man gently opened his eyes and delivered a heart-warming look in my direction.

"You have been on a long journey. Haven't you?" He said. "You must be hungry. Come. Let's go eat."

I was hypnotized by his presence. I silently conformed to his words and followed him out of the dome towards one of the wooden edifices established near the dome. There was a small garden with colourful flowers growing outside the cabin-like structure, which was constructed primarily of wood, with the foundation made of stones.

It was a silent walk to the cabin, which was minimal in its setting. We sat on some cushions placed on the floor next to a wooden table.

"Would you like some tea?" The man asked.
"Yes. Please." I replied.
"My students will soon bring some food for us. Till then, I will make tea for us." He commented.

The cabin had a fireplace installed in the corner, which is where the man made a fire and started the preparation for the tea.

"What is this place?" I inquired as the man boiled water over the fire for our tea.
"You can think of this place as an epicenter of learning and growing in the substance of self-realization." He replied.
"I see. And you are the teacher here?" I asked.
"One of them. There are a few of us. We like to think that we are both teachers and students." He replied with a genuine grin. "For individuals to become good teachers, it's necessary that they always stay curious and willing to learn."

"That makes sense, I guess. What do you teach here? This place is incredible, how did you even build it?" I asked with curiosity.
"I wasn't the only one who built it. There were several of us." He said. "In many ways, the space created itself. We decided to come together and live here to expand our consciousness and nurture our creative spirits."

"Everything that transpires in our lives is simply a by-product of what we become in ourselves." He narrated. "It is a mere reflection of who we are inside. For instance, in the reality you have just come from, people are consumed by darkness in their hearts. As a result of that, their actions have destructive tendencies attached to them. I think you are already familiar with this."

"Yes. I am." I said. "One of the reasons why I got on this path."

"And what path is that?" He asked, as he brought hot water and two cups with him to sit opposite me.

"A path of bringing light to the people in my reality. To remind people that they hold the strength in themselves to face the darkness that has currently gripped them, so that they can free themselves from their suffering."

"Hmm." He murmured, while pouring some tea for us. "You should stay here with us for some days. We have many children here. Most of them are orphans, whom we adopted. You could help us take care of them and in exchange, we will teach you whatever we can – to further help you evolve on your path."

"I found this place by accident as I was heading towards that peak, wanting to climb it." I declared while pointing my fingers through the window in the direction of the peak. "But something tells me that I was also brought here for this. I am certainly willing to be of service and stay here for some time to learn from you." I declared.

"Wonderful." He replied with a joyous smile as we sipped our teas.

A student soon walked in the room with freshly prepared food. "The food we eat is all grown in the fields here." The man said, while the student, who was a young man, placed the food on the table. He had a bright glow on his face.

"Thank you Dorjey." The man said to the young man, who bowed in return and left.
"What do I call you?" I asked the man.
"You can call me Tenjin." He replied with a smile.
"And you are?" He asked.
"James." I said.
"Great to have you here, James." He remarked. "Let's eat now."

Simply looking at his face made me feel elated.

We relished our senses over the course of that freshly prepared meal of vegetable stew and
rice while engaging in delightful conversations about life. Tenjin was very much familiar with the reality I had come from. It was like being in the company of an old friend, who I had mystically come across in an enchanting space hiding in a jungle.

I stayed in one of the many wooden boxes that were built along the trees. Most of the older students lived in rectangular boxes like mine, while the younger ones shared a common space. Somehow, this space acted as a capsule for me to integrate everything that I had been through. I followed a daily schedule of waking up at 5 am to meditate alongside the other students inside the dome. The sessions were led by Tenjin, who was a Zen master. He would guide us to focus our awareness on our breathing, in a mindful attempt to become one with the present moment. We practiced deep breathing and then observed our breath for a few hours in the morning. Tenjin instructed us to continue being mindful of everything that we did.

"Every action you partake in, make sure you are completely present in it. Be mindful of your every move. When you're walking, be aware of each step. While eating, be fully engaged in the act of it. Feel alive in each moment. Be as mindful as possible through everything you do, as if it was ensuing in slow motion." Tenjin would recite.

After meditation, we practiced body movements in an open space, where one of the other teachers, a fascinating woman named Rigzen, guided us to move our bodies in coherence with the energetic field within us.

"Experience the movement of the energy within. Your body isn't limited to the physical." She would tell us. "Let the energy flow in your body, to open your blockages and experience longevity."

We practiced all kinds of movements under Rigzen to embrace the fluidity of our bodies and find the deep connection between our breath and the energy that circulated around the body. I found the body movements to be a big release. Earlier,

I had a tendency to become chained by the endless streams of thoughts drifting in my brain. Connecting with my body through these movements was helping me break that chain. My awareness was being carried to all parts of the body, further enhancing my experience of being alive.

After engaging our bodies in the movements, we would have a meal together cooked for us by the people in charge of running the kitchen. Community was an important part of living in the jungle space and so, everyone in that community had different responsibilities based on what they liked to do and what they were good at. We would sit together in a circle and savour our time together.

Afterwards, I would perform one of my responsibilities – work in the fields, weeding them for a proper harvest. Few others would weed with me, teaching me how to do it properly while engaging in conversations and making me laugh the entire time we worked. I practiced being mindful through every action. Working on the fields with my feet planted over the soil always felt extremely nourishing.

Post this, we would take some of the harvest to the kitchen, where the kitchen people would prepare afternoon meals for us. I got some time to myself in the afternoon. During that time, I would go into the jungle to find a spot from where I could stare at the peak – my reason for coming here. Every time I saw the peak, I knew the day to climb it was nearing.

After watching the peak, I would go fulfill my other

responsibility – going to the jungle to collect wood. All the younger and older students generally came along. Tenjin had told me that most of the younger kids didn't have fathers, and that they simply needed a masculine figure to look up to. With time, I found out about the difficult circumstances that the younger kids were rescued from. Some had been rescued from sex traffickers. Some from abusive families. Some from villages that had been struck by environmental catastrophes that had destroyed everything.

I never had my own children but now that I was brought into this role, my fatherly instincts were jolted. I loved being with these kids – boys and girls both - and answering their million questions. Their curiosity and enthusiasm made me feel alive. Their ability to love and their innocence was simply beautiful to witness. It didn't matter if I wasn't biologically related to them. For me, they were like my own children. I saw no difference. I no longer saw the world as theirs or mine. I saw it as a collective union of everything coming together to play its part in life's symphony.

We would return from the jungle with ample wood before the sunset to have dinner together. After dinner, the whole community would sit in the dome to sing devotional hymns. Most of the hymns were in their native tongue, so I didn't understand them, but the purity of the vibrations being generated from their hearts were enough to get my heart devoted.

After the evening gathering, I would sit with Tenjin in his cabin to gain something out of his well of profound wisdom.

Being in his joyful company after an elaborate day of living was the most enjoyable part of my day.

Everything about him was simply exceptional – his humility and the grace with which he carried himself, his devotion towards the kids and his students, his understanding of the distinct realities, and his guidance on how I could do my part of bringing light into the reality I was born in.

"All of us have been born with a purpose instilled in our hearts. We are simply not aware of it because of all the layers that are in the way. Our purpose could be as simple as working in the fields to grow food, or teaching bodily movements to others; but no matter who we are and where we are born, there's a light in our hearts waiting to be ignited forever." Tenjin said to me one evening.

"So, purpose and light are the same thing?" I inquired, while sipping my tea and overlooking the luminous peak under the moonlight.

"The label of it doesn't matter, James. What truly matters is that there's a tremendous capacity in our hearts. By simply tuning in with that capacity and letting it expand, we can learn to live our truth by totally immersing ourselves in life." Tenjin clarified.

"What am I to do, if or when I decide to go back to New York?" I asked.

"I think you already know the answer to the 'what'. It's the 'how' that you will have to figure out. I am sure that with time you will be able to." He remarked with a gentle smile on his face.

"I have received so much in so little time. My being is changing exponentially every single day. Sometimes, I don't know how to deal with it. I just want to scream and share this abundance with the world so that they can experience a taste of what I am going through. Before, I was merely living in a cage. And now, I have been freed." I exclaimed. "Most people in my reality are still living in that cage. They have no idea what it feels to be alive. To feel the reckoning of our hearts. To witness our darkness and then be able to harness the light."

"That is why you are here, James. To train and deepen your understanding of the light and the dark so that when you return to your reality, you are able to live your purpose with full integrity and clarity." Tenjin declared.

"And when should I return? Or should I even return?" I asked. "I am happy here, and maybe I don't need to go anywhere."

"You will know what to do when the time comes. But one thing is certain, whatever it is that you are growing in, one day you will have to share it with others. The people in your reality need light. They are chained by darkness." He said. "Do you remember how you were before?"

"Yes. I do. I was miserable." I replied.

"There are people out there who are more miserable than you once were and they don't even know how to get out of their misery. When the time comes, you can be of help to them. You can be a source of inspiration." He said. "The world needs to find its balance. We need as many people as possible to bring light to your reality. The weight of darkness can only be lifted if an increasing number of people start facing their fears, look inwards, acknowledge their darkness and cultivate the courage to fight it."

We drank our tea as the night brightened in its luminous shade to bring out the potency of the mountains that were striking outwardly in an infinite expansion of a formless ray.

Months went by as I lived under Tenjin's guidance, training my being to elevate in its consciousness. I also took that time to dedicate my time to be of service to the kids and the community as a whole, who had readily accepted me as part of their own with open hearts.

With time, I wasn't thinking about climbing the peak. I was simply learning to embrace the teachings of Tenjin, immersing myself fully in the occurrence of every fleeting moment.

It felt like home in many ways. I hadn't even thought about Jessica or anyone from my past. I was so engrossed in observing the arrival of each novel breath that all of what I was or had done before and all of what I would be or do in the future didn't matter.

My entire way of operating was shifting while living in that jungle. Being crisply aware of the breath through meditation practices in the morning had sharpened my mind, while being mindful of each action had eventuated my being to enter another stream of living. Whether it was working in the fields, collecting wood with the kids from the jungles, celebrating in cohesion with everyone in the community or spending time with Tenjin, it was all part of a synchronized spectrum of coexistence, where I was purely engaged with everything that ensued in those boundless moments.

Nothing held much significance in my heart except the moments that presented themselves with an all-abiding generosity of a recurring dream, teleporting me to a world beyond the current one. My perception was changing every day as my eyes were starting to behold the material in five dimensional formations, tearing my mind from its limiting behaviour of solely being conscious in the three-dimensional world.

It was while I was sleeping one night that I heard Jessica's voice. Even though I was not conscious when it happened, it felt real.

I remembered the words of my father, who is to say that whatever happens in dreams isn't real.

In my dream, I was teleported to an altered reality. A place beyond the passageway. It was an infinite white space. Jessica was standing in the middle of it. I could get closer to her and our fingers could touch.

"Have you forgotten about me?" She asked in a teasing tone.
"I can never forget you." I declared. "You're the reason I am here. You're the reason why any of this has transpired. Without you, I wouldn't have left New York or that previous life of mine. Calling it a life would be an overstatement, considering I wasn't even alive through it."

"I knew you would find your way." She remarked with softness in her voice.
"Thank you for believing in me when I had given up on myself. If not for you, I wouldn't have realized the things that I have realized now. I would never have felt so much joy and gratitude. So much has happened. I wish I could tell you everything." I said.
"You don't have to tell me anything. I already know." She replied. "I can see you changing. I can feel it too."
"Really? You can?" I inquired.
"Yes. We are linked, James. Our spirits are tied together through a pure, inconceivable bond. It knows no boundaries and breathes through a legion of realities." She remarked.

"I now understand why you had to disappear. If you hadn't, I wouldn't have been able to realize the power of unconditional love. My heart has expanded." I said. "Even if I never get to unite with you, I am at peace knowing that my love for you comes with no conditions and it doesn't change if you are not with me physically. My heart will always love you no matter what happens."

"I love you, James." She said as her voice blended in the lightness of my awakened dream.

I woke up the next morning, knowing in my heart that it was time for me to climb the peak. Such was my resolve that even before sunrise, I got my things together and went to see Tenjin to let him know that I had to go.

"It is time for me to go." I said to Tenjin as he was walking towards the direction of the dome.
"Walk with me." He replied.
I silently complied.
"You will be going to that peak?" He asked.
"Yes." I said.
"Make sure to take everything you have learned here with you." He remarked. "People living in your reality need to be reminded of what truly matters in life."
"Yes, they do but I am not going back to my reality." I said.
"No one returns from that peak." He declared.
"I have heard that before." I commented.
"Then you must know that you are going on a one-way journey." He said.
"There's no other way. I have to do it." I declared.

I hugged Tenjin and thanked him for all that he had bestowed me with. The students were walking into the dome for morning meditation when I said bye to everyone. A touch of melancholy and surprise originated in their eyes on seeing me leave.

"Where are you going?" Some of them asked, while some stayed quiet.
"To that peak." I said as my fingers pointed to the summit.

The look on their faces communicated everything that was in their hearts. They knew that they may never see me again but that didn't affect the flow of energy among us, for we truly cherished one another.

I continued my walk through that jungle in the direction of the peak. My eyes were capitulated by water as the heart had unraveled on experiencing the treasures of human connection.

CHAPTER SIXTEEN

THE GOLDEN LEOPARD

The peak felt miles away as I hiked through the jungle. I felt great triumph as the last of the doubts about who I was and what I needed to do were erased. The yearning to climb that peak was a symbolic representation of the escalation my inner being had been undergoing.

The fear of not returning didn't cross my mind. My head felt clear with each soaring moment. The fear of death didn't consume me either, for I knew my spirit had deepened beyond the physical. It was at peace.

I didn't cross any more villages as I walked for days through the jungle. During the nights, I slept inside caves and ate wild plants. I learnt about which plants to eat from my time with the community in the jungle. The plants were native to these jungles and full of nutrients. They packed enough minerals in them to allow me to survive for days. I soaked my body in the chilling streams and engaged my lungs in deep breathing to enhance my physiology. The sun fuelled my cells with plenty of life force. Nature, in its truest and purest form, enriched my body, oxygenated my system and furnished me with enough strength to keep on progressing.

As the peak neared in sight, it started to get chillier. My lips and the skin on my face started to crack. I was aware of the pain in my body, but I was in no rush and gave my body time to rest whenever it desired. I had packed enough plants to feed myself for weeks.

In a week or so, the trees began to lessen in number and the terrain became rockier. I was starting to see glimpses of snow fields on the way. There were no trees blocking the expansiveness of the Himalayan range from my view. Infinite miles of empty land besieged me, with no other human in sight. However, there were many animals that were always more scared of me than I was of them.

I had a close encounter with a snake once when I was resting inside a cave. I heard it hissing as I was relaxing after a long day of walking. The fire had run its course and the cave was completely dark. My body was exhausted, but my mind felt awake. I knew it was a snake as soon as my ears apprehended the hissing.

I opened my eyes. It was pitch black, but I could hear the snake slithering. My eyes were able to make out its lengthened figure through the darkness. Its skin was shining. As I lifted my neck to look, the snake was gazing directly into my eyes. It was raised and static. I didn't say a word and tried to observe the fear that rose through my body, all the while staying detached from it. I felt capitulated by the snake's eyes and felt my body enter a state of hypnosis. I wasn't sure if the snake was going to bite me but something in me told me that it wasn't. Moments later, it slithered past my body and went further inside the cave through a slender pathway.

This cave must be its home. I thought to myself.

The snake accepted me as its guest and let me stay the night. I noticed this about most animals in that jungle. As long as I didn't threaten them in any way, they never tried to harm me. The more I practiced staying still and calm through everything, the easier things became. If I reacted to anything out of fear or anxiety, I was taken away from the present moment and instantly felt a dip in my vibration. In those moments, I quickly remembered Tenjin's teachings to bring awareness to my breath again. I would take a deep breath, let everything go with an exhale and simply become mindful of the unfolding moment.

"Be one with the wild. We are products of nature, not the other way around. The more in tune we become with all of life, the more we integrate with it." Tenjin would always tell me. "There's nothing you need to worry about when in the jungle. Animals and trees are your friends. You live in them as they live in you. The more you embrace the oneness of it all, the more you will be able to deepen your understanding of the self."

The teachings I received since I landed in Mumbai were being put to practice throughout my hike towards the peak. I was being confronted with everything that was left of me amidst the vacuum of that land. At some point, the terrain got more vertical with a heightened elevation that made it tough for the lungs to breathe and incited the body to be in a state of hypothermia. My toes were frozen, and I couldn't feel my palms or my face. I couldn't feel my body. My sensations numbed. I was forced to take strength from the life force in me to keep moving. I tried engaging my lungs in deep breathing to generate warmth from the inside. But just like in the desert, something in me kept me going.

My heart was pumping gradually, when I took a moment to simply look around the white that was spread throughout those mountains. I was reeling with bliss as I was reminded of another one of Tenjin's stories.

"There's a myth regarding the peak that you keep staring at." He said to me one night, as we were sitting inside his cabin, and I was looking at the peak.

"Is there? What is it?" I had asked.

"I can see the way you look at that peak. It is only fair that I tell you about the myth that has been prevalent in the valley for thousands of years." Tenjin had said.

I was listening intently.

"A leopard lives on those peaks." Tenjin had said.

"A leopard?" I had questioned. Even though I spent so much time in those jungles, I hadn't heard anything about a leopard yet.

"It is not an ordinary leopard, but a special one." Tenjin continued. "It is white in colour with lustrous golden spots spread across its body. It hides in the snow. It can see you, but you cannot see it. Many villagers believe that the leopard is the deity of that mountain, for if you see the leopard, you become free."

"Why haven't I heard about this leopard yet? I have been here for many months." I had said.

"No one talks about this. It's considered disrespectful." Tenjin had said.

"I see. And why is that?" I had asked.

"The villagers don't believe in calling names to their deities. It goes against their traditions." Tenjin had said. "No one has ever returned from that peak. The villagers believe that the leopard eats them, as an offering to keep peace alive in the valley. They are meant to be free now. The outsiders who visit this valley obviously dismiss this story and simply attribute the men not returning to the harsh weather conditions, which make it impossible for anyone to survive."

"Do you believe in this story?" I had asked Tenjin.

Tenjin had smiled.
"But if no one returns from the peak, how do the villagers know that there's a leopard living there?" I had asked.
"That's the real question, isn't it? How do they know? How do any of us know what we think we know?" Tenjin had replied in a mysterious tone.

"Hmm. I don't know." I had replied with a nod and a smile. "I guess we don't know much and what we do know is simply based on the stories we have been fed throughout our lives. Source of which is unknown."

"Yes... our lives are built around a collection of unending stories. So, what are we beyond those stories?" Tenjin had responded in an inquisitive manner.
"Beyond those stories we are nothing really…" I had said.
"Or we can be everything." He had remarked.
"But is there a difference between being nothing and being everything?" I had said.
"Is there really?" He had questioned.

I returned from my flashback with Tenjin, and wondered if there really is a leopard? If the myth isn't just a myth? Maybe, the story could be true after all?

I looked up but couldn't see the peak, as the walls of the mountain acted as barriers. I was still far from it and wasn't sure if my body would be able to make the climb.

A storm was surfacing through the sky, so I had to stay in a tiny cave for a few days. My body couldn't move an inch in those days. I was inside that cave, struggling to breathe and trying to stay alive. The storm was reckless, and I had made peace with the notion that my body might die in the cave itself.

I closed my eyes in harmony as my consciousness coasted away.

The storm subsided after a few days. My eyes unsealed to perceive the flickers of the sun shooting inside the cave. I gathered all the strength left in my body to pick myself up and walk out of the cave. The sky was blue and the sun was emitting its rays on the mountain. I let the sun energize me, as I trembled out of that cave. My body was numb. I didn't have any sense of physicality left in me anymore.

I gradually continued the climb, until I arrived in a bare meadow with a pond and some greenery around it. Just as I approached the pond to drink its nectar, I saw a white leopard with golden spots. Its image reflected in the water against mine. The sun was making the leopard's golden spots shine. It was the most surreal thing I had ever seen. The leopard came alive in the water. It was the Golden Leopard.

I couldn't believe my eyes as the leopard tenderly twisted its neck to look straight at me. I was on my knees, looking into the water. I was frozen, but the leopard was gazing at me. It was looking through me. I had never felt like that before.

I felt as if God was looking straight into my eyes. Not God

as we know or think of it through our conditioned means. But, unity as a whole is what I felt through that gaze. The entire universe condensed in a blasting moment of endless expansion.

The pond wasn't reflecting my face or body, but just the leopards'. Did that, then, mean that the leopard was in me, that God was in me? I marveled.

I tried to grab hold of the leopard as I dipped my palms in the water. The leopard disappeared, but my own reflection materialized in water.

I was thoughtless in that moment but everything made sense. It was all in me. The leopard. Jessica. Maya. My father. They were all in me. Every single being was in me. The entire universe was in me. And I was in everything.

In that brief but eternal moment of bliss, I realized that there was no separation of life. All existed through one source of union. There was no sense of "I" and no sense of "them". It was all just one, living through a funnel of infinite expansion.

My life felt fulfilled as frozen tears streamed down my eyes. I looked up at the sky and knew in that everlasting occasion that I was free - free from everything and nothing at the same time.

I drank the nectar out of the pond. It furnished my body with strength and from that point on, I didn't stop climbing till I reached the top of the peak.

It was just before sunset that I reached the peak. My eyes overlooked the breathtaking valley I had walked through. The sun was so near me, it was as if my palms could hold it. I could see the horizon from all angles, with the peak acting as the center of the universe.

I kept staring at the sun as it was setting. My body started collapsing with the dusk that was grasping the sky. I was trying to keep my eyes open to see the last bits of sun setting down the horizon, and as it went completely under, so did I.

I fell in peace to unite with the grave of snow that had been waiting to hold me tight.

My eyes gently opened, as I woke up to stare at a white ceiling. I was in my apartment in Chinatown, New York. I gently raised my body and noticed Jessica standing further in the distance. She was putting on a one-piece black dress over her beautiful, smoothened skin. An extended mirror was placed on the wall and she was looking at it while wearing her dress.

"Someone's been in a long dream." She remarked with a sly smile while using her palms to pull the dress up from her waist. She let the dress sit over the front of her body and the unzipped part be suspended in the direction away from her naked back. A protracted zip was left to be pulled from her lower back towards the neck.

I was in a disoriented state of mind, not knowing what had just happened. Had I just been dreaming all along? I asked myself.

"Do you mind?" Jessica said while pointing her eyes flirtatiously towards her naked back.
I got out of the bed to slowly zip the dress and let it cover her back. I gently kissed her neck and let my palms hold her waist. She turned around to swiftly kiss my lips.

I was still confused, not knowing what was going on but I was happy to be looking at her again.
I brought her close to me and embraced her as tightly as I possibly could.

"I love you so much." I declared to her as I let her body become one with mine.
"I love you too." She replied.
"So much has happened and I don't know how to make sense of it or explain any of it to you but my love for you has grown immeasurably through all of it." I declared.
"Whatever it is, you don't have to explain anything. I already understand." She whispered in my ear.

Tears of joy dripped down my eyes, as I kept holding Jessica. She held me tight, as I cried openly in her arms.

I looked up at her. She was smiling and looking back at me. It was unimaginable being with her. I didn't know what to make of anything yet. My mind was spinning in circles, and I stayed with my breathing, to simply be in tune with the present moment - the only moment to exist - just like Tenzin had taught me.

"I have to get going." She said.
"I don't want you to go." I replied.
"I know, but you have a lot to do." She said, as she pointed her palm towards the desk, where blank sheets of paper were retained.

An urge began in me to capture and write about the moments that had been my reality for as long as I could remember.

"Go get a shower and start writing. I will see you later." Jessica said.
"When do I see you?" I asked.
"Meet me at our diner, later?" She said.
"Perfect." I said.

She gently kissed my lips and left the apartment.

I jumped in the shower to awaken my cells and get a grip on what was happening. Many questions were still on my mind.

Had Jessica never disappeared? I asked myself. This story emerged since I started writing. But how could it not be true? How could it not be real?

I lived it. I felt it. It changed me. Everything did transpire. It couldn't just be part of a dream.

But then again, how is living in a dream different from being part of a reality? Why is it that our definition of what makes something real inevitably makes something else unreal?

I was smacked by the obscurity of that moment, but I wasn't chained by it. I felt free in myself. The teachings stayed with me. The meetings stayed with me. All those places stayed with me. The understanding of the world and my inner being stayed with me. The expansion of my heart stayed with me. The matured love in my chest for Jessica stayed with me. The connection with my father stayed with me. The Golden Leopard stayed with me. Everything that had transpired in the dream stayed with me.

How could I forget that moment of being one with the leopard, with God? How could I be the same person as before? For it may have just been a dream, but it was no less real than anything I had ever experienced before. Everything in me had changed. I was no longer the same person as before and I was happy to be embracing this new unfamiliar self.

I sat down on my desk after taking a shower. I couldn't stop writing till the sun set. One page after another; words poured in from a source beyond me. I was called in from distinct realities, to now arrive at a moment where I stood free from everything and could live as a channel of pure creation.

The truth of altering realities didn't matter as much as the moment I was in now. That was the only certainty that mattered. I wasn't questioning anymore. I was simply being. I was purely creating.

An acceptance for everything had surmounted my spirit and the questions pertaining to the obscurities of the day's happenings disappeared. I was simply flowing along with everything that was transpiring. I wasn't thinking about what was real and what was not. I was merely aware and present, living through the experience of whatever life presented itself with.

I left the apartment later at night to go meet up with Jessica. I walked past the place where Huan's store used to be. Instead of the shop, a pawn shop stood. I didn't think about Maya or any of the other people that had entered my stream of consciousness. They had all served their purpose to bring me where I needed to be now.

I strolled along the streets of New York. They felt livelier than ever before. I arrived at the diner, where behind the counter was the same waitress that had taken our order the first time Jessica and I had eaten together.

Jessica was sitting in our usual booth next to the windows, as I walked inside the diner to join her. I kissed her and sat opposite her.

"Welcome back, you two." The waitress said to us.
"Thank you! It's good to see you." Jessica said to the waitress. "Can we get two coffees?
"Two coffees coming your way." The waitress replied in a pleased tone.

The bar where Jessica used to work was located at the corner across the street. I glanced at the bar without pronouncing a word. I was observing the show, engaging when it seemed fit.

"I quit working at the bar." Jessica said.
"How come?" I asked.
"I got a lead role for a play on Broadway." She declared with euphoria in her eyes.
"Wow! That's wonderful." I replied delightfully. "You deserve it!"

It felt as if somebody had pressed the pause button from the moment Jessica had disappeared and now, they had pressed play again. But something deep inside me had changed this time. My consciousness was entirely different. I truly loved her, but not in the same way that I used to. I loved her just the way she was, in her divine self.

I felt sacred in my being, and simply wanted to share with her the companionship that aroused between us.

We sipped our coffees as I silently gazed at her striking face, feeling grateful in my heart for having found her. I had never actually lost her. She had always been next to me, while I had gone traveling through my mind to distant realities.

I was no longer consumed by the illusion of any reality. I was in sync with my breath and alive to each moment's calling. I was free from the shadows of my past, and grievances of my future. Love was brimming through my heart - for Jessica and for everyone around me. I had expanded in harmony with the universe, to share with others the light of my being.

For, I now knew that it was possible for us to emerge out of darkness and embrace our light. I had found what I was looking for, and I simply had to share it with others.

She was smiling at me, as I kept looking into her eyes, to be guided along on a path to bring light and love in this world.

THE CONTINUATION

There were many things I had to put in order, but first I had to let out the stream of words that were flowing through me. I barely left my apartment in the coming month. The blank sheets were being filled with impressions of my being's travel through distinct realities.

I didn't stop writing till there was nothing more to write.

The moment I finished, I visited my mother. I hadn't been to Queens since I had left, almost two decades ago. I didn't have any remorse in me as I was sitting on the train, on my way to Queens. It was early morning when I was standing outside my mother's house - the house I grew up in and despised for the longest time.

I walked to the door and rang the bell. I wasn't sure if my mother was home, but I was hoping she would be there.

My mother opened the door a few minutes later. Her face brightened as she saw me, and I couldn't stop myself from hugging her.

"I am sorry." I said, as I felt comforted by her warm embrace. "I haven't been the best son but now, I am here."
"There's nothing to be sorry about." My mother said. "You were doing what you thought was right."
"I met father and I am no longer afraid of being who I am." I said.

My mother held my shoulders and looked at me in silence. Her eyes were inquisitive.

"You met your father?" She questioned with confusion in her eyes.
"Yes. I know it's hard to believe but it's a long story. I will tell you some other time." I said with a smile.
"Come on inside, James." She said.

We sat in the kitchen and I was reminded of the time when my brother and I used to sit on the kitchen table as kids. My heart was open, I felt relieved to be sitting in my mother's company. She could tell something had happened but didn't ask further. She simply held the space for me to be. That's what she had done her entire life.

"I am grateful to have you as my mother." I said.
"Oh James… you have been such a blessing to me. My life changed the day you were born." She said. "You always had a good heart."

"I was lost for a long time, but now I understand what truly matters. It's the people in my life. It's what I can do to bring light to this world. It's not about being vicious but kind. Life isn't a competition. It's an exploration of the self and others that can only be done and nurtured through love." I said. "I lived in darkness for many years, but I finally get it now. And I am thankful for you to have given me this gift of life."

There were tears of joy in my mother's eyes. I spent a few hours in her company before leaving Queens for Manhattan and walked around the city, simply observing the movement of people.

In the coming days, I reached out to Samir.

> Dear Samir,
>
> I am sorry for not being there for you. I hope that one day you can forgive me. I abandoned you when you needed me the most. I was selfish and ignorant in my blind quest for the life I was trying to build, and it took me a few years of living through hell to finally arrive in this space of acceptance and peace.
>
> I wish to reunite with you and hope we can be brothers again. I am willing to do whatever it takes to heal the wounds that were left in our relationship through my actions.
>
> I hope you are well, and I hope to hear back from you.
>
> Love,
> James

I was picking up the broken pieces of my life and building it all over again from scratch, with the hope that I could be a force of good in the world, that I could act from a place of love and compassion to bring light to the world.

I was in love with Jessica, and I was falling in love with life, learning to live through my heart among the madness of New York City.

Things were starting to align in coherence with my intentions of bringing light in the world. Months after I finished writing, my manuscript was picked up by a publisher. It was to be launched in December of 2013.

Jessica and I were drinking our coffees, at our usual diner.
"I can't believe this is happening." She said.
"Me neither." I replied. "I have to thank you for everything. Without you, none of this would have been possible. You brought me back to life."
"The life was always in you." She said.
"Yes. But, if not for you, I wouldn't have discovered that for myself." I replied.

After finishing our coffees, we continued our walk along the sidewalks of New York. It was the day of the book launch. The event was being held in an exquisite space inside a trendy bookstore.

A rectangular shaped display stand stood with craftily designed words, "Book launch - The Broken Man, by James Walsh" ingrained on it. The display was placed outside the glass windows of the space.

There were many unfamiliar and a few familiar faces in the crowd as I began reading a prose from the chapter of the book. My mother and brother were seated in the front row, next to Jessica. Even Victoria and Adam had come for the reading. Both were seated separately in the back row.

"It is in giving life a chance that we learn to ride the wave of suffering. It is in our broken heart that we find the strength to heal. It is in our darkness that we grasp the essence of light. There were many instances where I thought I had it all figured out until I realized that it is in our not knowing that our humanity thrives. It is in our acceptance of chaos and uncertainty that our wisdom grows.

I have learnt many things over these last few years of healing my broken self. One thing I know to be true is that only love has the potential to heal us, to show us the power that we hold in ourselves.

If not for love, we wouldn't know what to live for. What to strive for. What to look for.

Love helped me heal, helped me understand that there are forces mightier than us governing our lives, persisting among us to teach us what truly matters in life. We can easily get lost amidst the distractions of today but that need not be our fate.

For it is on us to decide what we want for our lives. If we decide to choose love over hate and light over darkness, we will be able to fully live life as liberated and happy beings."

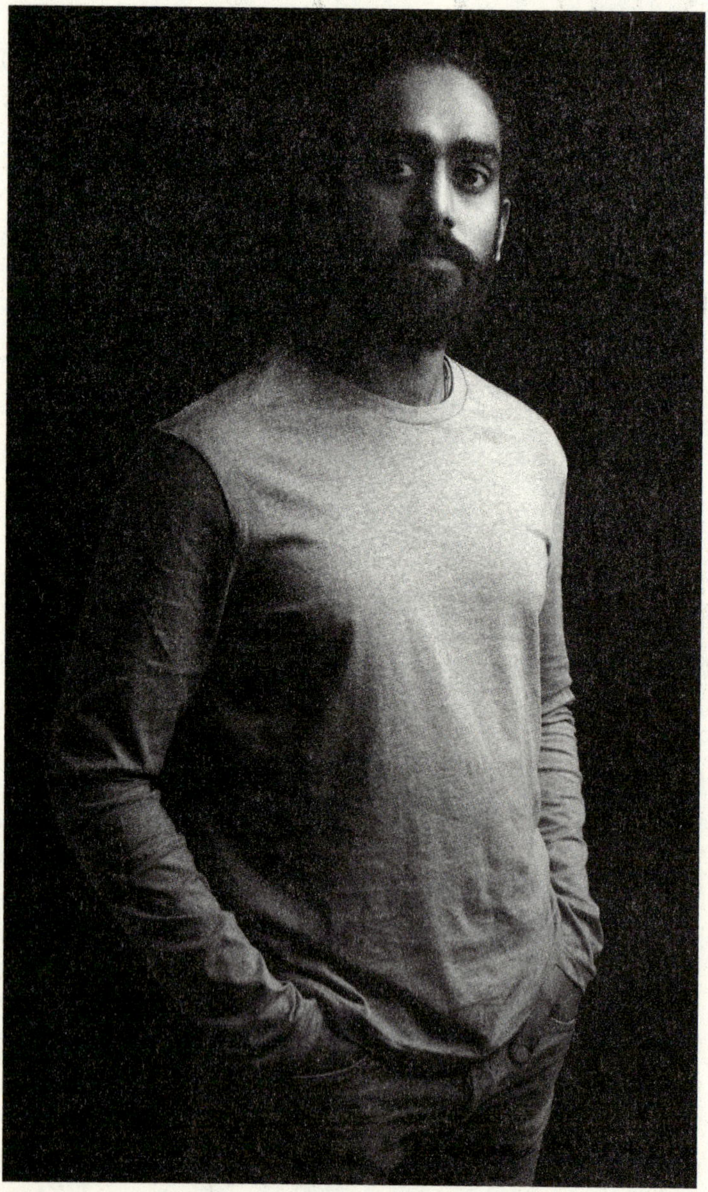

ABOUT THE AUTHOR

An accidental writer with an online community of thousands across the globe, Kartikeya Ladha first gained international recognition after the launch of his first book, Dream Beyond Shadows, in late 2018.

Dream Beyond Shadows became an Amazon Bestseller in India after capturing people's imagination with countless insightful stories based on Kartikeya's experiences during a life changing expedition to Peru, South America. The book created a path for Kartikeya to encourage thousands to embrace creativity and courage in their lives, to pursue self-discovery.

Kartikeya was born in Gwalior, a historic town in India, and grew up immersed in the richness of India's vibrant customs and family life. He was educated in a rigid educational system at The Scindia School, a relic of the British Raj era. After completing high school, he left India to attend Northeastern

University in Boston, U.S.A., where he concentrated on management and entrepreneurship.

After graduation, he moved to Brooklyn, New York, and worked for a solar start-up company as a door-to-door salesman, soon becoming a team leader. In one of the most successful community solarization programs in the United States, Kartikeya knocked on doors in Brownsville, an area tagged by TIME magazine in 2012 as "Brooklyn's Most Dangerous Neighborhood." He educated hundreds of households about climate change and motivated them to take positive action for the environment by embracing renewable energy. Kartikeya quickly became the company's highest earner and enjoyed all the delights of fast city-living, until an inner voice surfaced from the darkness, compelling him to renounce his long-held plan of building a life in America, and instead to seek the truth of human existence.

His quest for the absolute truth led him to walk an unknown path that inspired travels to faraway lands worldwide. He went beyond life's usual norms to unearth his calling in this magical world, by initiating an unending discovery of himself as a human being. Wanting to give life to a new work that exemplified the rawness of "what it means to be a human being," Kartikeya continued his explorations, returning to his home county, where he traveled into the heart of the Himalayas, facing extreme conditions and challenging his mind to gain powerful insights for its re-creation. This was followed by a solo pilgrimage on foot from Kanyakumari to Goa, where he walked more than 1000 kms in three months.

Kartikeya's travels within India inspired his second book, Life Unknown – A Passage through India, which continues the themes of Dream Beyond Shadows and goes further, taking the readers into the deep unknown, to face the darkness in life in order to be able to recognize the ever-blazing light that shines within them.

Now a successful author of two books, Kartikeya is continuing his journey as a writer, more importantly as a creator, to break his dimensional boundaries and give birth to new creations.

His new book, 'UnHerd', a fictional tale of love, wisdom and strength, is a result of a deepening self-realizing path that Kartikeya has been on, where the sense of the 'I' is breaking and a sense of interconnectedness can be seen in everything and everyone. Kartikeya is no longer on social media. He dedicates his time to connect with people in person and deepen his craft.

Other works by the Author